Hawaiian Holiday

A Jesse Ashworth Mystery

Stephen E. Stanley

Hawaiian Holiday

A Jesse Ashworth Mystery

Stephen E Stanley
Copyright 2018

Stonefield Publishing 2018

BOOKS BY STEPHEN E STANLEY

A MIDCOAST MURDER
A Jesse Ashworth Mystery

MURDER IN THE CHOIR ROOM
A Jesse Ashworth Mystery

THE BIG BOYS DETECTIVE AGENCY
A Jesse Ashworth Mystery

MUDER ON MT. ROYAL
A Jesse Ashworth Mystery

COASTAL MAINE COOKING
The Jesses Ashworth Cook Book

JIGSAW ISLAND
A Novel of Maine

DEAD SANTA!
A Jesses Ashworth Mystery

MURDER AT THE WINDSOR CLUB
A Jeremy Dance Mystery

UP IN FLAMES
A Jeremy Dance Mystery

ALL THE WAY DEAD
A Luke Littlefield Mystery

CRUISING FOR MURDER
A Jesse Ashworth Mystery

A GRAVE LOCATION
A Luke Littlefield Mystery

POTTERY AND POETS
A Luke Littlefield Mystery

MURDER AND MISBEHAVIOR
A Jeremy Dance Mystery

A PRAYER IN ORDINARY TIME
A Novel of the Home front

TRAILER TRASH
A Jesse Ashworth Mystery

WIND IN THE SAILS
A Jeremy Dance Mystery

MURDER ON SHAKER HILL
A Luke Littlefield Mystery

DEATH INSURANCE
A Jeremy Dance Mystery

A PRAYER IN TIME OF WAR
A *novel of the Home front*

ROAD KILL
A Luke Littlefield Mystery

MISSING
A Jesse Ashworth Mystery

A PRAYER IN THE DARK OF NIGHT
A novel of the home front

CHARACTERS IN THE STORY

Jesse Ashworth- *Retired teacher and part time detective*

Tim Mallory-*Retired chief of police and Jesse's partner in business and life*

Rhonda Shepard- *retired teacher, and owner of Erebus Gift Shop*

Monica Ashworth Goulet- *Jesse's cousin*

Jason Goulet- *Jesse's best friend from high school*

Jay Cummings-Ashworth- *high school English teacher and Jesse's son*

Jessica Cooper- *Tim's daughter*

Derek Cooper- *Bath chief of police and Jessica's husband*

Jackson Bennett- *owner of a local insurance company and Rhonda's fiancé.*

Steve Palmer- *high school math teacher and Jay's partner*

Johnny Chapman- *owner of the Torch Light Bar*

Travis Chan- *Honolulu homicide detective*

Peter Thompson- former *surfer and former owner of a classic VW van*

Donny Smith- *owner of a North Shore surf shop*

Lisa Takamoura- *wants answers to her brother's death*

John Smith- *known as Skippy, a waiter at Ruby's Restaurant*

Christine Drake- *wants to find her missing husband*

Stephen E Stanley

Author's Note:

This book is a work of fiction. All characters, names, institutions, and situations depicted in the book are the product of my imagination and not based on any persons living or dead.

Stonefield Publishing
Portland, Maine
2018

Stephen E Stanley

sometimes you need to step outside, get some air, and remind yourself who you are, and who you want to be.
                                                    -Anonymous

Chapter 1

It was another day in Paradise. I stepped out onto the lanai with my morning cup of coffee and took in the view. Between the buildings I could see sections of Waikiki Beach and to my left I could see Diamond Head. The calendar said it was February, but to me it seemed like an endless summer. Sitting at the small table and sipping my coffee, I remembered why I was here.

It had taken me almost a week to get here. I could have done the flight all in one day. I also could have jumped off a twenty story building, but that didn't appeal to me either. To break up the trip I had stopped in Las Vegas for a few days and then on to San Francisco to see the sights before hopping on a jet to Honolulu.

This wasn't my first time in Hawaii. I had been here three times before when I was much younger. I loved how it seemed a different world and how far away it was from daily life. It had been a rough year. On my birthday no less the doctor had called me to say, "Mr. Ashworth, there seems to be a problem with your blood work, and I'd like to see you in my office as soon as possible."

I knew that wasn't good, and when he informed me that I had a form of chronic leukemia he told me not to panic. In most cases it never develops to the stage where it needs to be treated and other than a checkup every six months I should be fine.

I was fine and then I wasn't, so a six month ride on the chemo therapy rollercoaster had just ended. I love my hometown of Bath, Maine, and all my friends there, but I needed to get away by myself and recover both physically and spiritually. The fact that I hate winter with a passion helped the decision along.

My partner Tim Mallory and I run a small security agency back home. It's called the Bigg-Boyce Security Agency because we bought it from Mr. Bigg and Mr. Boyce, but the locals call us the Big Boys Detective Agency. Tim and my two friends Hugh Cartier and Jason Goulet are finishing up a case back home, and then I expect everyone will head here and leave the agency in the hands of my son Jay and Tim's daughter Jessica and her husband.

I planned to be here for the winter, so I rented a condo rather than a hotel room, and I had a kitchen to cook for myself if I didn't feel like running off to a restaurant, but so far I've enjoyed eating out and not cooking, except for breakfast. My typical breakfast is cereal, fresh fruit, and yogurt. And coffee of course, good local Kona coffee.

I've heard that people after chemo sometimes have an identity issue, and I believe it. I feel like I left myself back home, and here I'm someone else, but I don't know who. But the one thing I know is that I don't feel whole.

It was time to start my day, which be pretty much like every day: eat, swim, walk, nap, read, and repeat. *Aloha!*

Last night as I was having an umbrella drink in a nice open-air bar news stories were playing on the bar's television. There was a three day blizzard in the Northeast from Washington to Nova Scotia. I thought Washington needed a good blizzard or two, but I felt bad thinking that back home the snowplows, generators, and snow blowers would be working overtime. So bad in fact that I ordered another drink and then went for a walk along the beach.

The one thing I love about Hawaii is the diversity of the people. Nobody cares much about what you are or what you look like, and it's a great place for people watching. I had left my inhibitions back home, too. I never wear shorts in public back home, but here I would feel overdressed in long pants. You wouldn't catch me dead in a Hawaiian shirt back home, but this was, after all, Hawaii. One of the first things I did was head over to Hilo Hattie's and buy some shirts, but I bought muted designs and colors so I wouldn't look like a tourist, and then I packed away all my New England clothing. I draw the line at flip-flops. I bought a pair of sandals. In an emergency, how could I ever run in flip-flops?

Finishing my coffee, I showered, got dressed, and headed out the door. Something told me to vary my morning routine. I should point out that that "something" is a little voice in my head that tells me to pay attention to my surroundings. I've learned over the years to listen to my sixth sense and that to ignore it doesn't end well for me.

I should explain that my cousin Monica and I had been taught by our grandparents to listen to our inner voices. We come from a long line of Spiritualists, and though we don't practice Spiritualism and are basically skeptics, we are more sensitive to our surroundings then other people.

So instead of heading to the beach I walked down Paki Avenue to Kapiolani Park. It was early and the place wasn't busy. Later in the day many locals would be picnicking in the park, and tourists would be wandering around looking for that authentic Hawaii of their imagination.

There were parked cars along the way and I wondered where their drivers were because the automobiles were unoccupied. Walking along I spotted a red Volkswagen camper from the 1970s. There was something about the van that made me pause. I hadn't seen one for a long time and I noticed that the windows were open and the curtains closed. I love cars and as I walked along I was able to recognize different automobile makes and models.

I had a sudden craving for coffee, so I headed out of the park and up Kalakaua Avenue until I found a small coffee shop and had a cup of coffee and a tasty pastry, and watched the people as they passed by on the sidewalk.

My phone went off and I looked at the caller ID and sighed. The ID read Clyde Ashworth, so it was either my father or my mother. "Jesse," said my mother on the other end of the line, "is it true you ran away from home?"

"No, Mother, I didn't run, I took an jet plane."

"I called your office and Jay said you went to Hawaii? Are you looking for hula girls? There are plenty of girls here in Florida. You should have come down here."

"Mother, we've been over this. I'm not looking for hula girls or any girls. And I think we now call them women by the way."

"Did you get tired of your detective hobby? I remember you playing detective with that tin badge when you were a kid. Maybe you should go back to teaching."

"I'm retired from teaching these last twelve years, and Tim and I aren't indulging in a hobby. The agency is a real thing."

"Who's this Tim?"

"Tim Mallory. Remember, we grew up together. He's my partner."

"Has he found a woman yet?"

"Put dad on the phone, please," I needed to touch reality again.

"CLYDE!" she yelled into the phone. "Jesse wants to talk to you."

"Hello son. You're mother is crazy as a loon."

"I'm not crazy!" she yelled in the background. My father ignored her.

"How are you son?"

"My blood count is normal, so it looks like the chemo worked."

"That's good news. I'm glad you were able to get away for a while. You must be worn out."

"He needs to get a real job," yelled my mother from somewhere in the house.

"Yes, I admit I feel beat up. Thankfully everyone understands I need some rest. How is mother by the way?"

"Good days and bad days. The doctors are confident that her problem is plaque buildup in the arteries to the brain. They are going to operate and open them up, and hopefully that will help."

"Keep me updated," I said. "Love you both," and I ended the call.

I think it was Bette Davis who said "old age ain't no place for sissies."

Chapter 2

It was evening and I was sitting in a cozy tiki bar I had found beyond the tourist area. The bartender, Johnny Chapman, had taken a liking to me and treated me to a free umbrella drink. He was a well-preserved fifty year-old with dark hair and bright blue eyes who, like me, was a New England native. He had grown up in the next town over from Bath. He had come here on vacation and never went home, and he was a great source of local information.

"I'm looking for an authentic curio shop," I told him.

"I know just the place," he said and wrote down the address for me. "They have some unusual items you won't find anywhere else."

"Perfect."

"I'm off tomorrow," he said. "You want to grab some lunch? I know some places the locals go where they have good, authentic food."

"Sounds great," I replied.

"We can meet here for a drink around noon and then head out for lunch."

Just then I caught something on the television above the bar. "Turn that up," I said pointing to the television. On the screen was the red VW van I had noticed on my walk in the park. According to the news report the van hadn't moved in several days and when the police went to check they found a body in the van. The police determined the death was suspicious, but the name of the victim was being withheld.

"What's going on?" asked Johnny, curious as to why I was interested in the story.

"I saw that van this morning and had an uneasy feeling about it."

"Interesting," he said. "Does this happen to you often?"

"You've no idea," I replied as I finished by drink and munched on the pineapple piece from the empty glass.

I arrived at the Torch Light Bar at noon the next day and Johnny was already there. I grabbed a seat next to him at the bar and he nodded to the bar tender who produced a bay breeze, garnished it with fruit and placed it in front of me. "My treat," said Johnny.

"Thanks, but you are too generous."

"I own the bar," he replied. "I can do anything I want."

"Nice bar. I was looking for Hula's Bar and Hamburger Mary's," I said wistfully, "but they seem to be gone."

"They've been gone for some time. I guess you haven't been here for a while."

"I haven't been here since 1988. Funny, much of the area looks the same, but the hotel names have changed. When did you arrive?"

He looked around before speaking. "I came here in 1990. I was living in Boston with my then boyfriend. When we broke up I moved as far away from him as I could. Why did you come here?"

"I came here during the summer. As a teacher I loved my job, but it was so spiritually draining that I needed the summer to refresh myself. Coming here was stepping into a different world. I loved being here on the Fourth of July and watching the outrigger races. So when I finished chemo treatments, I needed somewhere to refresh myself, and this was far from the world of oncology."

"And you're okay now?" he asked.

"My blood work is normal, so treatment was successful, though there is no cure. They are developing new treatments, so I'm hoping for a healthy future."

"That's good news," he said.

"So don't get me wrong," I said wanting to satisfy my curiosity, "but you run a bar and meet men all the time…"

"Let me stop you right there," he said before I could turn the thoughts into words. "You are very good looking for an older man, and you have a brain, and you are from home, and I get the sense that you don't want anything from me. You've no idea how many men hit on me because I own a bar."

"I imagine free drinks are on their mind. Plus you are good looking, so it's a win win for the booze crowd."

"You got that right," he responded. "Now tell me something about yourself."

"Not much to tell. I grew up in Bath, as you know. I attended college in Boston, and got my masters at the University in Southern Maine. I taught English at Amoskeag High School in Manchester, New Hampshire for thirty years, and when my best friend Rhonda moved to Bath and opened a gift shop I followed her to help her set up her business. I had no intention of remaining there, but when I arrived I met up with all my old high school friends and decided to stay. Then I met the chief of police, Tim Mallory. We had grown up together, and we reconnected and in no time he moved in with me. That's about it."

"There must be more than that," he said.

"Well, Tim and I bought a security agency and we've done some detective work," I admitted.

"You're too modest," said Johnny. "I did an internet search on you, and you and Tim seem to be good at missing persons and solving murders."

"I'm on the internet?" I asked. I've never really thought about it.

"Yes, and you've written several cook books. You must be a good cook."

"I cook and I think people just like to eat. I do have good recipes, which I think is the secret to good cooking," I speculated.

"For most of my cooking," said Johnny, "I use Hawaiian recipes."

"That must be interesting," I said, "though I'm not all that fond of poi."

"Poi, I think, is an acquired taste. But Hawaiian cooking is much more than poi."

"And," I admitted, "I've never been to a luau."

"Really? I thought that most tourists had to experience a luau."

"That's just it. I think most of them are for tourists. I saw the Kodak Hula Show on my first trip here, and that was it for touristy stuff."

"Me, too," he agreed. "But there are many authentic things to do here…" His phone rang and he looked at the caller ID. "I need to take this." He excused himself and took the phone call.

As I watched him he seemed to go pale. "Something wrong?" I asked him once he returned to the table.

"You know that red van you saw in the park?"

"The one with the murdered person in it?"

"That person," he said looking pained, "was Bill Takamoura, a very good friend of mine."

Chapter 3

When I woke up from my afternoon nap I called Tim. It was already night time in Bath because of the time difference, and I still had the rest of the day ahead of me.

"Argus misses you," Tim said about my pug dog.

"Just Argus? I asked.

"Argus and everyone else. Monica says you have a murder situation there."

"I haven't spoken to Monica in a few days."

"Monica said she had a feeling. Both you and your cousin scare me sometimes."

"You signed up for it," I reminded him. "And how often has my intuition helped us out in a case."

"Your intuition, as you put it, borders on witchcraft sometimes."

"Boo!" I said into the phone. Then I told him about the red van. "When are you flying over here?"

"Jason and I have a few more alarm systems to install and we're working on a divorce case."

"Well hurry up, I miss you," I said.

"We all miss you, but I think Rhonda will be the first one to fly out there."

"Is she bringing Jackson?" I asked. Jackson Bennett is her long term fiancé.

"She said Jackson can't get away from his insurance business. But I think she just wants to have time alone with you."

"And Hugh?" I asked. Hugh Cartier was a police detective in Montreal whom I met when I was living there studying at a cooking school. He's been a good friend.

"He has gone back to Canada to do some business. He'll probably fly out there when he's done."

"Well, I can't wait to see you all" I said. "I'll let you go because I know it's late there.'

"Love you," he said.

"Back at you big guy." I ended the call. I sat back and thought of Tim. Tall and handsome and built like the proverbial brick house. No one in his sixties should still have six pack abs like that and a full head of hair still sandy-brown in color with only a few streaks of gray.

I thought of calling my son Jay, but as I looked at the clock I figured as a teacher he would have gone to bed early.

Putting on my swim trunks and tee shirt I headed out to the beach. Back home Maine has some lovely beaches, but survival time in the North Atlantic water is about five minutes and I hate cold water. Here the water is warm and the waves are wonderful. I first learned to do a modified form of body surfing here years ago, and still loved having the waves pick me up and escort me back to the sandy beach.

I'm not a sun worshiper, and I can't think of anything more boring than lying in the sun with nothing to do, but give me a lounge chair in the shade, a book, and an ocean view, and I'm a happy man for hours. Add a shirtless pool boy bringing me umbrella drinks and life is perfect.

I walked along the crowded beach with my feet in the surf and carrying my sandals, and it felt good to be alive. I headed back to the condo to jump in the shower, change and decided to check out the curio shop Johnny told me about.

The address wasn't familiar to me, so I knew it was probably in downtown Honolulu. I waited for the bus and found myself in a quaint older part of town. The curio shop was easy to find because the window was full of handmade tikis, silver candle sticks, odd shaped mirrors, and various other decorative objects I couldn't identify.

I was looking for gifts for those back at home. Viola Vickner, our local Pagan priestess, would be taking care of my dog Argus when Tim flew out to join me. I wanted to get her a nice handmade tiki. There were three other customers browsing the merchandise as I entered the shop. It appeared to be a popular place for locals as well as tourists.

"Are you looking for anything in particular?" asked the older gentleman behind the counter who appeared to be of Asian descent.

"I'm looking for a tiki statue as a gift for a friend of mine," I replied. "She's a Pagan and appreciates religious objects from other cultures."

"I have just the one in the back room. It's hand carved by an island artist." He disappeared into the back room and returned with a tiki that was about a foot in height.

"This was carved from wood that came from the Big Island. It's heavy," he said as he passed it to me.

I reached out to take the tiki and felt a burning sensation as I touched it. The sensation made me drop it on the counter. I must have exclaimed something because everyone turned around to look at me. "I felt a burning pain when I touched it," I said to explain my dropping the object.

"You felt the heat?" asked the older gentleman, "But you're not Hawaiian."

"Yes, I know that," I said somewhat annoyed.

"You must be a spiritual teacher because the tiki spoke to you."

"Actually I was a English teacher. I'm afraid I don't understand."

"The tiki recognized you as a Kuhuna, a priest or a spiritual leader. That's why you felt something when you picked up the statue."

"Is there any way you could ship that to the mainland?" I asked. I wasn't about to pick it up again.

"Of course," he said. I wrote down Viola's address, paid for the object and got out of the store as fast as I could. I've been called many things, but this was the first time I'd been called a Kuhuna.

It was happy hour when I arrived back in Waikiki, and I headed over to the Torch Light for my afternoon drink.

Johnny was behind the bar. "Jesse, I have someone I want you to meet." He called over to his bar helper to take over mixing the drinks, and he took me over to a table where a young woman was sitting by herself.

"This is Jesse Ashworth," he said to the woman. "This is my friend Lisa Takamoura. She's the sister of my friend Bill, the one who was found murdered in his red van. Jesse here is a detective back home."

"How do you do?" she said. "Pleased to meet you."

"And you also Miss Takamoura," I responded.

"Please call me Lisa," she said. "Please both of you sit down." We sat down and I had a fairly good idea why Johnny wanted me to meet her.

"Lisa would like your help in finding out who killed her brother," said Johnny getting right to the point.

"I see," I said. "Aren't the police working on the case?"

"Of course," said Johnny, "but Lisa wants to make sure they are on the right track."

"I would suggest," I stated, "that you find someone local who knows the island. I am really only a stranger here."

"Johnny said you have a good record," Lisa said speaking for herself. "So I did some research and you seem to have an ability for solving problems. I also know that not all of your cases are local for you. You've solved crimes in Canada haven't you?"

"Yes," I admitted. "But I usually have help."

"I'll help you," offered Johnny. "I know the area and the people."

"Again," I said trying to think of a way out, "why not let the police handle it?"

"This may seem like a big city to you," said Lisa Takamoura, "but ninety percent of the people here are tourists, so in reality for the locals it's a small town, and I would prefer to avoid gossip. And I'm willing to pay."

"Which means," added Johnny, "that you can afford to stay on the island longer."

"I'll give it a shot," I said preferring island breezes to winter blizzards."

Chapter 4

Homicide detective Travis Chan signaled me to take a seat. "Now Mr. Ashworth, what makes you think you can solve a murder better than the Honolulu police?"

"I make no such claims, Detective Chan," I replied. "I've been asked to look into the case by the family." I couldn't place Chan's ethnicity. With a name like Chan I had expected to see a man of Asian descent, but his makeup appeared to be predominately Caucasian and something else, and like many multiracial persons, he was strikingly good looking.

"What was the cause of death?" I asked.

"He was hit over the head with a blunt object."

"Any chance he fell and hit his head?" I asked. "Someone could have seen him fall and helped him into his van and he could have died shortly after that."

"The injury," Chan explained, "was too violent to have been the result of the fall. His head was basically smashed up to a bloody blob." I tried to suppress the unpleasant image from my mind. Chan continued, "Well, as it happens I know Johnny Chapman and since it was his friend who was murdered I'm willing to share whatever I find with you under one condition."

"And what would that be?" I asked.

"That you share anything you find out with me."

"Agreed," I said.

"Good. I'll be at the Torch Light around five after my shift. Here's a copy of the report,"

"Yes, thank you Detective Chan."

"Call me Travis," he said. "I'll see you for drinks later."

What was that about? A homicide detective wants to meet me for drinks at a gay bar? And he's giving me a copy of the report? It's true I've worked with the police before, but that is usually because Tim Mallory, as a former chief of police, is extended courtesy by "the brotherhood."

I was hungry despite the fact that I think my body was still on Eastern Standard Time, or maybe I just like to eat. I walked along towards the park and saw a food vendor and ordered a musubi, that strange rice, spam, and seaweed concoction. I don't understand the attraction to spam, but it actually wasn't that bad. I did wash it down with a cola though.

Having satisfied my desire for food for the time being, I headed back to the condo for a nap. Later, off in the distance I could hear the traffic as I slowly woke up. I remember my visit years ago to Kauai and the beach hotel where the waves on the beach lulled me to sleep. A week after I left the islands the hotel was destroyed by a tropical hurricane. I sat and read through the file on William Takamoura. There wasn't much there that Chan hadn't told me.

I looked at the bedroom clock and freshened up and headed out to the bar to meet with Detective Chan. I might be early or I might be late because I packed my watch away and was on Honolulu time. *Mahalo*.

Johnny was at the bar and I told him I was meeting Travis Chan. "He and I are *Hoaloha*."

"In English?"

"Friends. I called him earlier and he assured me he would work with you," said Johnny as he passed me a mai tai. It was strong when I tasted it.

"I'll have a beer," said Travis Chan as he took the stool next to me at the bar. Johnny must have seen him come in because he had the beer ready. "How are you Johnny?"

"Hoping you can catch Bill Takamoura's killer," said the bartender as he placed the glass of beer in front of Travis.

"I'll do my best," said Travis. "But you know how it is."

"Yes, too much crime and too few police officers," replied Johnny, like he'd heard it before. "Which is why you need Jesse's help."

"I'm not sure how helpful I can be," I protested. "I haven't worked a case alone before."

"You won't be alone," replied Travis. "I'll be working with you. Now, Johnny if the bar can spare you, let's go find a booth and you can tell us about Takamoura."

Johnny signaled to his helper to take over and then took us over to a booth in a quiet corner. "William Takamoura," began Johnny, "was born on the island, went to college on the mainland where he stayed for a few years before returning to the island. He worked here on Oahu at a surf shop. Never married. He was a nice guy."

"And how did you meet him?" I asked.

"His sister worked here, and he used to come in to see her. He was straight in case you are curious."

"That means nothing," said Travis. "I'll bet half your customers claim to be straight."

"Point taken," replied Johnny. "Anyway he and I became friends, and we hung out often with his sister."

"Any enemies that you know of?" I asked Johnny.

"Billy? Not that I know. Everyone loved him."

"Obviously at least one person didn't love him," said Travis.

"What's the story of the red van?" I asked.

"No idea," said Johnny.

"I checked," added Travis. "The van was registered to him. And he has owned it for several months."

"News to me," said Johnny.

"Something tells me we need to look at the van," I said.

"I've got the techs going over the van for any clues," said Travis. "We'll have to wait for a report. I need to get back to work. I'll be in touch, Jesse."

"He's a good cop," said Johnny after Travis left.

"I'd hate to work homicide," I said. "It shows you the seamy side of humanity."

"Did you check out the curio shop yet?" asked Johnny to change the subject.

"I checked it out and the experience was, well let's say different."

"How so?"

I related the story of the burning I got when I touched the tiki. "And then they all looked at me and called me a kuhuna."

"The islanders are very spiritual people," explained Johnny. "They recognize the gifts of others. Now tell me what all this is about."

"I was raised in a Spiritualist family. We were taught to use our intuition and talk to the dead," I decide to be blunt about it.

"And do the dead talk back?" asked Johnny.

"I have no idea," I said. "I'm at heart a skeptic, but if a feeling comes over me I go with it. I rationalize it by saying that my brain works differently by taking in context clues and presenting them as intuition."

"And you are satisfied with that simple explanation?" he asked.

"Not really," I admitted. "I try not to think about it too much."

"Can you predict the winning lottery number?" I've been asked that by skeptics all my life.

"Not as easily as I can tell that your brother died in a car accident," I said as the vision popped into my head.

"How could you know that?" asked Johnny as a shocked look crossed his face. "Holy crap!"

Chapter 5

I was sitting on the lanai reading Charles Dickens *Great Expectations* for the umpteenth time. Once an English teacher, well you know. The house phone rang and the doorman informed me that Travis Chan was on his way up.

"Travis, come in," I said as I opened the door.

"Thanks," he said as I pointed toward a chair. "Nice place. I've never been in a condo hotel before."

"The best of both worlds," I said. "Your own place, but a front desk, doorman, and maid service. I guess you don't get a lot of murders in a place like this."

"You'd be surprised," he said as he kicked back and looked comfortable in the chair.

"I was about to make some coffee," I said continuing the small talk. "Would you like some?"

"That sounds great," he said. I headed off to the small kitchen and came back with two cups of hot coffee.

"Let's sit outside and enjoy the air," I suggested. The lanai was big enough for a couple of lounge chairs and a small table set.

"Nice view," he said. "The Ala Wai Canal is nearby isn't it?"

"Yes, just a half a block back," I said setting down the coffee mugs. "It's quieter back here in this part of the city."

"The Caribbean is nearer for you, I'm surprised you didn't go there."

"I love the Caribbean, but my health insurance is only good in this country, and I didn't want to be too far from medical attention." I went on to explain that I had just finished chemo and wasn't feeling confident enough to be too far away from a major hospital.

"Are you cured?" he asked as he looked at me with concern.

"There is no cure for chronic leukemia," I explained, "but it responds to treatment and my blood work is normal." I wasn't sure why all this interest in my background.

"Sorry, it's just a habit to interview people. I hope I didn't offend you."

"Not at all, but I am trying to put it all behind me," I said as I looked at him. "The truth is I'm trying to get my footing; I've been knocked for a loop. What they don't tell you is that chemo messes with your head. I'm trying to find my identity again. I feel like I'm someone else." I wasn't sure why I was unloading all this on a stranger. Oh, well.

"I came over to share the findings the techs got from the van," he said adopting a more business like tone.

"I'm not sure I know the murder weapon," I said. "That wasn't in the report."

"We don't have the murder weapon, and it appears he was killed in the van."

"Was the van parked there near the park, or was it moved there by the killer?"

"That's a good question," remarked Travis. "We're not sure. We're checking any of the surveillance cameras that might be in the area."

"So you don't have much to go on," I added.

"No, but I'm going to go interview the sister if you want to come along later."

"Of course," I said.

He looked at his watch, "I need to get back to the office. I'll pick you up tomorrow morning around nine."

"I'll be ready," I said as I walked him to the door.

I looked at my phone as the caller ID popped up and my ringtone made an annoying sound. "Jesse," said my cousin Monica, "How are you doing?"

"I'm resting and relaxing," I said into the phone. "And you?"

"Cursing you as we dig out from the blizzard here. Over two feet of snow in twelve hours."

"A few clouds in the sky and gentle surf here."

"I'm thinking of a word that begins with 'F' and a phrase that ends with the word 'you'."

"Be nice," I said as I looked out over the city to a view I'd never get tired of looking at.

"So tell me about the cop," she said out of the blue.

"What cop?" I knew I hadn't said anything about Travis Chan to anyone back home.

"Let's see," she said stretching out her words, "you move back to Bath and take up with the chief of police. Then you go off to Montreal and meet Detective

Inspector Hugh Cartier. And now you've run off to Honolulu where there's been a murder, so of course you've met a cop. You have a thing about cops. It's an obvious pattern."

"I do not," I said emphatically, "have a thing for cops."

"I'm sorry, let me introduce myself. I'm your cousin and we share a semi-psychic background. You can't bull shit me."

"Such sarcasm," I said but I had to laugh. "I should know better than to try to have any secrets from you." And I told her about being asked to help with the investigation.

"I'm going to guess that he's good looking. For some reason guys find you attractive. I don't see the attraction myself," she said. Monica and I are very close and sometimes I think she really can read me too well.

"So when are you and Jason flying out here?" I asked.

"As soon as he and Tim finish up the job they are on. I should let you go. Talk to you later," and she ended the call.

Travis Chan pulled up in front of the condo building at exactly nine o'clock. I was outside waiting and enjoying the gentle breeze off the Pacific. I opened the passenger door and jumped in. "Good morning," he said as he pulled away from the curb. "I brought you a coffee." He pointed to the coffee cup in the cup holder. "Cream, no sugar, right?"

"Thanks." I said. "That's right." I was impressed that Travis noticed how I took my coffee. I guess paying attention to details is a requirement for being a good investigator. "So where does the sister live?"

"North shore," he answered. "She was a champion surfer when she was younger. Have you been to the north shore before?"

"Yes, I've been all over the island when I was first here years ago."

"What's your favorite Island?" he asked. "I assume you've been to several of them."

"I like the Big Island. It's not as built up as the others. But I'm not a fan of Maui, I have to confess. Seems like a honeymoon resort to me. On the other hand, I think Kauai is beautiful, so it's a tossup."

"I grew up on Maui," he said. "Back then it didn't have the resort vibe it has now."

"The thing I loved on Maui," I said trying to get my foot out of my mouth, "was the drive up to Haleakala." I had taken dozens of pictures of the extinct volcano crater when I was there in the eighties.

"That's still a place I visit when I go back to Maui," he said as we drove on. "Okay, this is her house." Travis parked in the driveway. Lisa must have been expecting us because she was waiting at the front door.

Chapter 6

Coming from New England I'm used to substantial houses that are built as shelter against the cold. Here the houses are much more open and built to keep out the rain rather than the subzero winds of the North. I wondered briefly how it would be if you've never seen snow in person. I know it looks pretty on a calendar. But calendars never show dirty slush, or salt caked cars or the number of deaths that are storm related.

Lisa's house was a pleasant surprise. It had a wide porch that looked out over a lush tropical garden and palm trees. On the porch at one end were several colorful surfboards. "Welcome," she said as she pointed to a comfortable seating area on the wide porch. She went back inside and came out with three glasses of tropical fruit juice. I took a sip. It was wonderful tasting, but I couldn't place the types of fruit. "How can I be of help?"

"When did you last see your brother?" asked Travis.

"Two Sundays ago," she answered. "He usually picks me up and we go to church and then out to brunch afterwards."

"And last Sunday?" I asked.

"He called and said he had something else to do," she answered.

"Did he do that often?" asked Travis.

"Sometimes, but he usually would tell me in advance. This time he phoned that Sunday morning."

"Tell me about the red van," I wasn't sure where the van fit into the picture.

"I never knew anything about a van. It was a surprise to me."

"He registered it six months ago," Travis informed her.

"He never said anything about it," she said looking confused.

"Did you notice anything about his mood in the last few weeks?" I asked.

"He seemed upbeat. He said he had a chance to make some money."

"Did he say how he was going to do that?" asked Travis.

"No, he didn't."

"Well," said Travis getting to his feet, "thank you for your time. Here's my card. If you think of anything, let me know."

"I will," she said as she stood up and offered her hand.

"We didn't learn much," I said to Travis as I slid into the passenger seat.

"Actually, we did. We now know he was involved in something that would make him some money. You want to come over to my place tonight for dinner? We can go over the case."

"Ah, sure," I said taken by surprise.

"Good. I'll pick you up around six tonight."

"I'll be ready," I said wondering what was going on.

Resting up back at the condo, I was falling asleep when my phone went off. "Jesse, what the hell is going on with you?" It was my best friend Rhonda Shepard. "I haven't heard from you in over a week."

"Has it been a week?" I asked innocently. The truth was I hadn't given much thought to the time. One day seemed like another.

"Are you okay? Do I need to drop everything and fly out there now?"

"I'm fine," I replied. "I guess I'm on island time. Time just slips away."

"If I know you," she said, "you've already gotten involved in something."

"Well," I admitted, "there was a murder, and I've been asked to look into it by the victim's sister."

"What a surprise. Can't you even go on a vacation without stumbling over a body?"

"It's not like I'm causing the murders," I protested.

"Anyway, I'll be flying out there in two weeks. I've already made my reservations."

"You'll love it here," I told her. "No snow, no frost, no ice and no problems."

"That's what you said about the Caribbean cruise we all took, and look what happened. Well, I'll let you go. Call me!"

"I will," I promised and then ended the call.

Travis Chan picked me up at six, and drove us to a part of Honolulu that I wasn't familiar with, which wasn't difficult because I stayed mostly in the Waikiki area. He had a small house surrounded by a tropical garden. I wondered how he could afford a house like this on his pay scale. Property on Oahu was astronomically expensive. As if reading my mind he said, "This house has been in my family for generations."

"This is very nice," I said as I looked around. The carved and ornate furniture pieces were probably handmade Hawaiian antiques. "Something smells good," I said.

"I was just putting dinner on," he said. "Would you like a drink?"

"Gin and tonic would be most welcome," I said as he pointed me to a chair.

"Coming right up," And in no time I had a drink in my hand. Travis had made himself a drink and took the seat opposite me. I wasn't quite sure why I was here and couldn't think of anything to say. Fortunately Travis began the conversation. "I'm hoping this is the last case I work on."

"Why is that?" I asked.

"I'm retiring after more than thirty years on the force," he said.

"You don't look that old," I said.

"I'm older than I look, and I'll bet you are too, though you don't look over late forties."

"Liar," I laughed and then told him my real age.

"I'd never guess that, but we are the same age."

"What will you do in retirement," I said. "I began a second career."

"I think I'll do what you do and become a private investigator."

"It's actually a great job. You can take only those cases that interest you."

"And," he added, "I will be my own boss."

"And no one can fire you," I said.

"Come in the kitchen while I make dinner." The kitchen was a surprise. It looked like something out of the 1920s. The refrigerator was on the small side with a round motor on top, and the stove was an old gas stove covered in green enamel. On the stove was a huge wok.

"I feel like I'm stepping back in time," I said as I looked around.

"That's the idea, though it has all the modern amenities hidden." He opened what looked like a wooden cupboard and it was a dishwasher. Another cupboard hid a freezer.

"I love it," I said. "I love to cook, and I've set up my kitchen something like this, but more on the English style with an Aga cooker. And I love the bookcase with cookbooks."

"I like to collect cookbooks," he said as he added ingredients into the wok. "And I have a copy of *White Trash Cooking* by Jesse Ashworth."

"I'm flattered," I said. "Though I hate the cover."

"I like how you are sitting on the steps of a trailer in a tee shirt and flip flops. You look the epitome of white trash."

"Not my favorite look," I said. "What are we having? It smells good."

"It's a Hawaiian specialty, spam and cabbage stir-fry."

"I've read how you Hawaiians love spam," I said.

"Wait until you see what I make you for breakfast," he said with a smile.

"Breakfast?" What?

Chapter 7

Breakfast was a spam and egg casserole that Travis threw together along with fresh brewed Kona coffee. He brought the casserole over to my condo early in the morning and finished it in my oven. It was surprisingly good, and we had breakfast out on the lanai. "It's a little on the chilly side this morning," said Travis as he looked around at the view.

"Seventy-five degrees is not chilly," I said. "You want chilly come to Maine in February. I'll bet the high temperature there today is a balmy eighteen degrees."

"No thanks," he said.

"That's how I feel, too." I said. "No thanks."

"I thought we would go over to Takamoura's place of work."

"The surf shop?" I asked. "Isn't it a little early?"

"Better to interview them before they get busy. We don't want to interfere with business."

Just then my phone beeped with a text message. It was my son Jay checking on me. I texted back that everything was fine. It dawned on me when he asked if I was okay, that I hadn't thought about being sick or having chemo in almost a day. I guess that was progress.

"Everything okay?" asked Travis.

"Just my son checking in on me."

"I didn't know you had a son."

"Neither did I until he tracked me down a few years ago," I explained.

"That must have been strange," remarked Travis.

"Very strange, but in a good way. We are trying to make up for lost time. More coffee?"

"More coffee would be great." After a second cup of coffee Travis and I got into his car and headed to the north shore. I'd never been in a surf shop, mostly because I don't surf. It looked like fun and if I were younger, I think I'd love to learn to surf.

The shack was pretty much like I thought it would be. It looked like something from a TV show: rustic shack and colorful surfboards and an older hippie type proprietor.

"I'm Detective Chan and this is my associate Mr. Ashworth," said Chan.

"I'm Donny Smith. You must be here about Billy," he said. He was tanned and wrinkled from years of sun. Something we in Maine never had to worry about.

"When did you last see Takamoura?" asked Chan.

"Like I told the police the first time, it was the day before they found him. He didn't show up to work and didn't answer his phone."

"What do you know about the red van?" I asked. For some reason I had a feeling the red van was a major clue.

"He's had it for a few months. He bought it off a dude who comes here a lot."

"Do you have the dude's name?" Travis whipped out a notebook and was ready to take names.

"Peter something," answered Donny. "I'll have to look up his name on some old receipts."

"We'll wait," shot back Travis. "It might be important." Donny Smith pulled out a box of paperwork from under the counter. To me it looked like a disorganized mess, but he easily pulled out what he needed.

"Peter Thompson," said Donny reading off the name.

"Address?" asked Chan. Donny read off the address as Travis wrote it down. As soon as Travis had the address we excused ourselves.

"Something about Smith bothers me," I said as a sudden feeling hit me. "You might want to look into his background."

"I think you might be right," he said. "Now I need to report to the station. I'll drop you off at your condo."

A fresh cup of Kona coffee and a good book on the lanai was all I needed to relax and unwind. Usually when I'm working on a case I have the urge to hurry and finish, but it must be the island vibe because I was just taking life as it comes. When my phone went off it snapped me out of a reverie and I hit the green button.

"Jesse, thank you so much for the tiki," said Viola Vickner on the other end of the line. "It's wonderful."

"Glad you like it, and I'm glad you're going to look after Argus when Tim flies over here."

"I love that dog," she said. "Now tell me about the tiki. I could swear it's alive sometimes." Viola was a local Pagan priestess, so I knew she wouldn't be surprised by anything.

"When I picked it up," I said, "it burned my hand. Everyone looked at me like I had just pulled a sword out of a stone. I knew then that the tiki was special, and I knew you would know how to use it."

"I would expect nothing less from you. You and Monica have tapped into the Great Universal Spirit."

"I don't know about that, I just think things happen," I said being uncomfortable with the topic.

"Whatever gets you through the day, Jesse. I'll let you go. Bright blessings!"

"And bright blessings to you also," I said and ended the call.

I sat the phone down and realized I had an urge to cook. I took that as a good sign that maybe I was beginning to turn back into myself. I called Johnny at the bar and asked if he was free to come to dinner. He said he was. Then I called Travis and asked if he was free, which he was. I was looking forward to cooking for them, but I also had a plan. It would be a good time for Travis and me to ask Johnny more questions about Billy Takamoura without making it seem like an inquisition.

I had found a small market with fresh produce and incredibly high prices, which I learned was typical of Hawaii, after all almost everything had to be imported.

Travis Chan was the first guest to show up. "Something smells good," he said as he handed me a bottle of white wine.

"I'm a New England cook," I said. "So don't expect spam and poi."

"Funny guy," said Travis as I passed him the cork screw.

Johnny Chapman arrived and he, too, had a bottle of wine. 'Do I smell pork roast?" he asked.

"Pork loin roast," I answered.

"I forgot you were a New Englander, too," said Travis as he passed a wine glass to Johnny. "I'd like to go there sometime."

"It will be very different," said Johnny. "And don't go in the winter."

"Or you could be stuck there in a major blizzard," I added.

"I just saw on the TV this morning that the Northeast is having another major storm," said Travis.

"They will all be cursing me back home," I said, but it all seemed so far away now that home almost seemed unreal.

Chapter 8

By the time we opened a second bottle of wine everyone's tongue seemed to loosen up. I was complemented on dinner which I chalked up to hunger and wine. I've been told I'm a good cook, but the fact is I like to cook and people like to eat, but when I watch a TV chef prepare a meal, I want to throw out my kitchen mitts, along with all my pots and pans.

"So tell us about Takamoura?" Travis asked Johnny as we sat in the living area after dinner, finishing up the wine.

"Not much to tell. He comes into the bar once or twice a week. He usually orders the same drink, gin and tonic."

"Does he ever socialize with the other patrons?" I asked.

"Sometimes, but he's not there to pick up guys. As far as I know he's straight," answered Johnny.

"Isn't it a little unusual for a straight guy to be at your bar?" asked Travis.

"Not really," said Johnny. "It's rare but it does happen. Some guys like to be admired by other guys. It strokes their ego."

"Is it possible," I asked, "that someone might take exception to a straight guy in their territory?"

"It possible," admitted Johnny, "I've heard such comments when straight tourists wander into the bar.

After all some guys go to my place because it's a safe place to be themselves."

"What else can you tell us?" asked Travis. "Has he been acting different lately?"

"Now that you say that, yes."

"In what way?" I asked .

"He was spending a lot of money on things, and I know he doesn't make much at the surf shop," explained Johnny.

"What type of purchases did he make?" Travis asked.

"Well, the red van for one thing. That camper van is a classic and that wouldn't have been cheap. He also bought an expensive camera and a laptop."

"Has anyone checked out his apartment?" I asked Travis.

"Yes, I had a team over there, but we didn't find anything of interest on his laptop."

"Well, in light of the new information we've gathered," I said to Travis, "it might be wise to take another look at his apartment."

"Probably a good idea," Travis agreed.

"He also has a room at his sister's house," Johnny informed us.

"I didn't know that," said Travis. "That might be worth taking a look."

"And we still have to interview this Peter Thompson person, too," I reminded Travis.

It was early the next morning when my father called. "Jesse, I just wanted you to know that your mother made it out of surgery and is recovering."

"That's good news," I told my dad. "Do you think she'll be better?"

"They are hopeful that the fog will lift, though your mother is, well, bat shit crazy."

"But amusing sometimes," I said to ease my dad's mind.

"Life is never boring. I'll let you go. I'll call you tomorrow and give you an update."

"Okay," I said. "I'll talk to you then."

For some reason I felt like I needed to call my cousin. I punched in her number. "What's going on?" I asked as soon as she answered.

"It's Jason," she said. "He's down with the flu."

"Your husband," I said thinking back, "picked up every cold and flu outbreak back in high school."

"He had his flu shot and he's on medication, so he is feeling better." Another thing I hate about winter are the colds and sniffles that go along with being imprisoned indoors,

"I hope you're okay and didn't pick up any illnesses."

"I'm fine. So how is your hot cop?" she said changing the subject. "Did you sleep with him yet?"

"What type of question is that?" I asked annoyed.

"I'll take that response as a yes. How is your murder case going?"

"We're only at the information gathering stage," I answered. "And I'm not getting any impressions either."

"Funny, when you said that just now I saw a pineapple pop up in my mind."

"A pineapple? That's interesting," I replied. As soon as she said that I had a feeling she was right. "I'm not sure how that helps, but I have a feeling you might be on to something." One thing I knew was that he wasn't killed with a pineapple. How embarrassing would it be to be killed with a tropical piece of fruit anyway?

After I hung up I looked at the clock and realized that Travis Chan would be picking me up in a few minutes so we could interview Peter Thompson together.

Travis Chan once again took me through parts of the island I'd never seen before. Travis had called Thompson, so he was expecting us when we rolled up to his house.

"*Aloha*," he said as we got out of the car. "Come on in so we can talk. The neighbors don't need to know my business."

His house was small and looked very tropical with bright flowered prints on the sofa and chairs.

"I heard about poor Billy on the news," said Thompson as he offered us fresh coffee. "What can I tell you?"

"When was the last time you saw Billy?" Travis asked between sips of coffee.

"Must be more than a week ago," stated Thompson. "I had stopped off at the surf shop for a new pair of trunks and Billy was working."

"You sold him the van didn't you?" I asked.

"Yes, about three months ago."

"How did he pay for it?" asked Travis Chan.

"He paid cash. Twenty-five thousand dollars," Thompson replied. "A VW camper van is a classic, and that was a good price."

"What was your relationship to Billy?" asked Chan.

"Casual. I saw him at the shop, and we surfed together a few times, but we weren't close or anything."

"Why did you get rid of the van?" I asked out of curiosity.

"I needed the money," said Thompson. He waved his hand around the room which I guess meant that he had expensive taste.

"Thank you for your time," said Travis as he put his coffee cup down and got up from the sofa, which was my signal that we were leaving.

"Anytime I can be of help," said Thompson as we said goodbye.

"What did you think?" Travis asked me as soon as we got in his car.

"I don't see a motive there. He's probably not our guy."

"I have to agree with you. Well, I guess we'll have to keep looking," he said as he pulled onto the main road back to Honolulu.

Chapter 9

The airport was busy as I paced back and forth waiting for the flight from Boston to unload its passengers. Slowly people began to emerge from the jetway. He was one of the last ones off, and he waved when he saw me. It was February school vacation and my son Jay had flown out to spend the week.

I had picked up a flowered lei at one of the lei stands and slipped it around his head as I moved in to hug him.

"How was the flight?" I asked as we headed for the luggage area.

"Long. You had the right idea breaking up the flight."

"I'm sorry Steven couldn't be here," I said. "But your partner had other things to do as I understand it."

"Yes, he was asked to visit his parents. They pulled the old 'this might be the last time' number."

"Let's get you back to the condo where you can take a shower, get fed, and crawl into bed."

"Sounds good, Dad," said Jay.

"There you guys are," said Travis Chan as he met us at the luggage area.

"Jay, this is detective Travis Chan," I said introducing them.

"I've heard a lot about you," said Travis as they shook hands.

"Funny, Dad didn't say anything about you," said Jay looking from me to Travis.

"We're working on a murder case," Travis explained.

"I'll give you the details later," I said.

"You know," said Travis to Jay, "You are the spitting image of your father."

"So I've heard," remarked Jay.

"Poor kid," I said.

Travis dropped us off at the condo. As Jay showered I called down to the restaurant for takeout.

"Am I getting a new daddy?" asked Jay smirking as he came out of the shower.

"Very funny," I replied.

"He is very good looking," offered Jay.

"Really? I hadn't noticed." Liar, liar pants on fire! I thought to myself. "Now get dressed dinner will arrive soon."

"Take out? Have you given up cooking?" asked Jay in mock horror.

"Yes, for the duration."

"How are you really feeling?" he asked concerned.

"Well I…" and then his concern broke my reserve, and I collapsed on the sofa with tears running down my face. "I'm so tired and I don't know who I am anymore."

"I've heard the term chemo brain," said Jay giving me a hug.

"Yes," I laughed feeling better that Jay was here, "It's a real thing. And I'm very glad you are here."

"But you are feeling better?"

"Yes, much better. I think eventually I'll be my old self again."

"Well, I miss the old you," said Jay. "And I'll do anything to get him back."

"Just give me the space and the support to climb back out of the abyss. Now get dressed. Dinner will be here soon."

Having Jay with me made me miss home, which I took as a positive step. We had a breakfast of pancakes with coconut syrup and linguica sausage in a nearby restaurant, Jay said he was going to head to the beach and get some sun while Travis and I checked out Billy Takamoura's apartment.

I was already beginning to think that Takamoura was living beyond his means by the fact that he paid cash for a classic VW van, but when I saw his apartment it confirmed my suspicions. There was no way he could afford the apartment working in a surf shop. I had to remind myself that I was working for Lisa Takamoura and not the Honolulu police department, which meant that I needed to report to Lisa anything that we uncovered during the investigation.

The apartment was in a modern building that included a gym and a pool, and a view of the city from the lanai. The kitchen had stainless steel appliances with stone countertops; the living room was richly furnished, and the bedroom had not only a big round bed, but also had mirrors on the ceiling.

"Where did he get the money for this?" asked Travis as we poked around.

"That is an interesting question," I said as I looked around. Something caught my eye. It was the painting above the sofa. Something about it made my inner voice begin shouting. I had been wondering if the chemo had affected my intuition, but it had returned loud and clear. "I think your boys missed something in their investigation." I walked up to the painting and took it off the wall. On the back side of the canvas was a dust barrier that I ripped open. Inside was a little black book.

"You found something?" asked Travis, though it wasn't really a question since I was holding it up.

"I think we know how he got his money," I said as I flipped through the book. I tossed the book to Travis and he began looking through it himself.

"I can't believe the tech team missed this," he said.

"They were more focused on finding blood stains I bet."

"As it is," he said, "this opens up a whole new line of questions."

Travis and I stopped at the condo to pick up Jay, who was sporting a mild sunburn. We headed over to the Torch Light Bar for a drink before lunch. Johnny Chapman was working the bar and I introduce Johnny to Jay. They shook hands and we ordered drinks. The place was busy but we found a table and Johnny turned the bartending over to his second in command and joined us at the table.

"How's the case going?" asked Johnny.

"We are making progress," I said, but I let Travis take up the narrative as I wasn't sure how much information he wanted to make public.

We were talking when suddenly the room became silent. It was such a jarring change that we looked around at why the room was quiet. "Oh my god!" someone screamed.

"That's Ian Stoddard, the movie star!" said Jay with reverence in his voice.

"Check out his entourage," I said. With Stoddard were two of the best looking guys I've ever seen. They spotted an empty table in the corner and headed over to it.

"I better go take their order," said Johnny as he got up, went to the bar to get a pad and a pen and went to the table.

"Check out the corpse in the wedding dress," said Travis as an elderly couple came through the door and headed over to Stoddard's table. She was at least well into her eighties with blonde hair and a flowered Hawaiian wedding dress with a big floppy hat. The man with her was equally old and was wearing a Hawaiian shirt that matched her dress.

Johnny took their orders and then came over to our table. "Want to go to a wedding?" he asked.

"Why not," I said. "This could be interesting."

Chapter 10

It was a great afternoon for a wedding, warm with a tropical breeze. We gathered on the beach to watch the wedding and joined some tourists who had gathered to watch the show. Ian Stoddard was wearing a hat and dark glasses and no one who happened upon the wedding would recognize him. I knew of course who Ian was, but I had never seen his films.

The couple had gathered a group of strangers to witness their vows and there were about a dozen of us present. Talking with the extremely handsome stranger as we gathered I learned he was a California anthropology professor, and that he had grown up in my home state of Maine. The couple, he told me, had been married decades ago and had just reunited. Supposedly the bride had worked in Hollywood as a stand in for Marilyn Monroe. I had a hard time picturing her as looking anything like Marilyn. Then again I was becoming acquainted with the toll that aging takes on the human body.

The wedding reception consisted of all of us trooping over to a row of food trucks and then sitting on the beach eating the food. It was a very strange wedding. Looking at the pretty men in the wedding party I wished it had been a shirtless wedding.

"It's really true about California people, isn't it?" whispered Jay to me.

"It would seem so," I agreed.

Travis and I left the wedding party early to begin checking out the information we had gathered from Takamoura's apartment. Jay said he was going back to the condo and sit by the pool, and Johnny went back to the bar.

"He was running what looks like a prostitution business," I said looking through the black book.

"It's in some type of code, though not all of it," added Travis.

"Do you recognize any of the entries?"

"There are a few places mentioned here that are interesting," said Travis. His phone went off and he excused himself to take the call. When he came back I could see that something was up.

"Something has happened," I said as I looked at him.

"The manager of Takamoura's apartment building called. Someone has broken into his apartment."

"Looking for this, no doubt," I said holding up the black book.

"Let's go," Travis said to me.

Returning to Takamoura's apartment we were confronted with the sight of a home in disarray. Drawers had been pulled out and emptied, tables and chairs had been overturned, pillows had been slit open, and pictures ripped off the walls. "Good thing we found the book before someone else did," I remarked.

"We need to check and see if there are security cameras in this building."

"I'm going to guess that Takamoura's 'employees' have their own keys to the apartment. This is probably where the action takes place," I said.

"What makes you think that?" asked Travis. "Intuition?"

"The mirror over the bed for one thing."

"That makes sense, I guess," Travis admitted.

Just as we were about to leave I had one of those flashes of intuition I had been used to dealing with all my life. "I need to check something out before we leave."

"Is this one of your psychic episodes?" asked Travis.

"Who said anything about psychic?" I asked wondering where that question came from.

"It came from your son Jay. He told me about your family being big into the occult."

"They were Spiritualists, not psychics," I clarified.

"What's the difference?" he asked.

I ignored the question and headed into the kitchen. Surprisingly the kitchen was more or less intact. It looked to me like the vandals were either interrupted by something or they ran out of time. I closed my eyes for a moment and concentrated and then walked over to a small crock on the kitchen counter that held various kitchen tools. I turned the crock upside down and all the tools spilled out onto the counter. There among the spilled tools was a computer thumb drive. I held it up in triumph.

"How did you do that?" asked Travis looking like he had seen a ghost.

"Common sense," I replied hoping he would be satisfied with the answer.

"I see," was all he said.

We headed down to the lobby and spotted the security cameras. We found the manager and he took us to the storeroom where the security recorders were. We pulled the DVD out of the recorder and Travis wrote out a receipt for it and gave it to the manager. "Is there a DVD player at your condo?" asked Travis.

"Yes, I haven't used it, but I'm sure it works. Let's head over there and see if it works," I suggested.

We arrived at the condo where I found a note from Jay, saying he signed up for a tour of the island. I fixed us a gin and tonic and I slipped the DVD into the player. I hit the fast forward button until the time stamp read today's date. We watched as the camera caught us entering the building earlier in the day. About an hour and a half later we saw ourselves leaving the building. Between the time of our first visit and our second visit there were several persons who left the building, but no one entered the building.

"What does that mean?" I asked. "No one came into the building except us."

"It means whoever broke into the apartment was already in the building before we first arrived. We need to check out the video of the people who left the building."

We set the playback in slow motion and watched as several people exited the building. The angle of the camera was set to show visitors as they entered. The angle was all wrong to see the faces of those who left. "Freeze the recording," I said as something caught my eye.

"What is it?"

"The temperature today is what eighty degrees or so?" I asked.

"Or a little warmer."

"What do you notice about that woman?" I said pointing to the screen.

"Oh, I see," said Travis. "She's all bundled up."

"Yes, she has a hat, a long coat, and dark glasses, but we can't see her face in any detail."

"I'm going to go out on a limb here," I said, "and say she doesn't want the camera to see her, which means…"

"That she was the one who trashed the apartment," finished Travis. He got up and hit the eject button on the machine and took the DVD. "I'm going to go back to the building and ask the manager if he recognizes the woman."

"Okay," I said. "Let me know if you find out anything."

"I'll call you if I do."

Chapter 11

What had I gotten myself into, I asked myself. Here was a case that promised to be a complicated mess, and I was in the middle of it all. I came here to rest and recuperate and now I was working on a murder case in Paradise. Then the truth hit me like a ton of bricks. I hadn't thought about chemo, or being sick in days. This is what I needed to get my mind off the last horrendous year.

I left Jay a note to join me at the Torch Light when he got back from his sightseeing tour. The bar was mostly empty; the working crowd had yet to appear. I sat at the bar and Johnny put a drink in front of me.

"I took a chance that you might want a gin and tonic," he said as he added a lime to the glass as he passed it to me.

"Just what I need," I replied taking that first sip.

"How's the investigation going?"

"Like a Russian nesting doll. You open one clue and there's another one, and then another one, and..."

"Yes, I get the idea," Johnny said.

"I'm going to meet Lisa Takamoura here. She is my client after all. I'm going to go sit in the corner. Send her over if I don't see her first."

"You won't have to wait long. Here she is now," he said as I turned to watch her walk into the bar. She looked around and I waved her over.

"Hello, Jesse," she said as she sat down. "How is the investigation going?"

"We are making progress," I answered vaguely. I wasn't sure how to tell her about her brother's business.

"Your brother," I said trying to see how much she knew, "lived way beyond what his job at the surf shop paid."

"I know. I asked him about it once, but he said he had investments. Is that true?"

"You better have a drink first," I said as I waved over to Johnny. He promptly brought over a gin and tonic for her, and a fresh one for me.

"Is it drugs?" she asked.

"No. Did he have a drug problem?"

"I've never known him to do drugs. Anyway, I think you're stalling. Tell me the truth."

"We think he was running a prostitution ring," I said.

"Prostitution?"

"Yes. You had no idea?"

"That would be the last thing I'd think he was involved with. Are you sure?"

"Yes, we found his records. Detective Chan is checking out the records we found."

"Do you think this is why he was killed?"

"So far it's the best clue we have."

"I can't believe it," she said. "I'm going to need some time to process this. How much do I owe you so far?"

"So far your retainer has covered everything," I said.

"Let me know when you need more money."

"I need to write all this up in a report and get it to you."

"Take your time," she said. "Just keep me informed."

"That is my job," I told her. She finished her drink, thanked me, and left.

Finishing my second drink while waiting for Jay to show up, I figured I needed some coffee. When I was young I could drink three cocktails and not feel anything. But now two drinks in two hours were too much. I've never had a hangover in my life, and I wasn't about to start now.

I was lost in my own thoughts and didn't notice Jay enter until he sat down at the table. "How was your tour?" I asked as Johnny brought over a drink.

"I'd only seen the profile of Diamond Head. I was surprised to see that it's a huge crater."

"And Pearl Harbor?"

"It was interesting to be there with Japanese tourists," answered Jay. "It was difficult to imagine what it was like on that day. And I just can't picture the Japanese as enemies."

"Or the Germans for that matter," I agreed. "I guess it's just as well. We have our own memories. I was teaching on September 11th."

"Me, too. It was my first year of teaching."

"I remember walking through the cafeteria and it was eerily quiet. The students were shocked and I think confused."

"I was shocked and confused," added Jay. "How is your investigation going?"

"I could use your help."

"You need my help?" he asked in amazement.

"I don't have Monica here to bounce ideas off. I could use a second pair of eyes. And I know you've inherited the family insight."

"Insight? Is that what you're calling it?" he laughed.

"Is witchcraft a better term?" I asked amused.

"More colorful anyway. But I don't think we want to invade Viola's territory. What can I do?"

"I usually start by writing out information on index cards. Later on I can arrange them in order and shuffle them around. It usually helps."

"And then you and Monica go psychic with the cards."

"Go psychic?" I asked.

"It's a theory."

"Okay," I said as I took out my stack of index cards. "Billy Takamoura was found dead in a classic red VW van."

"Do you think the van is important?" Jay asked as I filled out the first card.

"I think so, but I'm not sure why. Next card. Detective Travis Chan is assigned to look into the murder. We interview the sister. She hires me to look into the case."

Jay put his hand on the card when I finished writing on it. He closed his eyes and said, "Why hire a private detective and not leave it up to the police? There must be a reason for it."

"According to her, she wants to make sure the police are on the right track," I said and even as I said it a voice in my head told me to pay attention. "She hired me, I think, because she suspected that there was more to the case than the police would look for."

Jay nodded in agreement.

"The next part is puzzling." I said. "When I went to the police station to get an overview of the murder, Travis Chan decided that he and I should work together."

"You been a consultant before," Jay reminded me.

"I know, but usually it's an official request. This time it's just a personal request from Chan."

"I think he likes you," said Jay, half joking and half serious.

"I'm not young anymore."

"But you don't look your age. Neither of you do."

"Anyway," I said to get back on track. "Next card. Bill Takamoura, who is believed to be straight, hangs out at the Torch Light."

"Some men are vain enough to want to be admired, no matter who does it."

"Yes, we've all seen that," I agreed with a yawn. "Still…"

"Dad, you are tired. We can continue this tomorrow."

"Well…" I was conflicted. I wanted to finish the cards, but I was dead tired. "I guess you are right. Let's get some take out dinner and head home."

Chapter 12

Another day had passed and I hadn't used algebra once. In fact I hadn't used it in at least the last 16,425 days. But then again there were probably math types out there who had never read Shakespeare. I pity them. *Aloha*.

Jay had made breakfast and then took off for another day of sightseeing. I couldn't blame him. At the end of the week he would have to return to the frozen New England weather and school.

I was having my second cup of coffee when I got a call from Travis Chan. "I'm going to Hanauma Bay and do some snorkeling. Want to come along?"

This took me by surprise. "Sure, why not?"

"Great. I'll pick you up around ten."

"I'll be ready." I was glad that I had gotten some sun and wasn't so white that I'd stick out in bathing trunks like a tourist just off the plane. That reminded me I needed to call Tim. I punched in the number for the detective agency, and Jessica Cooper answered.

"Hi Jesse," she said. "Good to hear from you. Are you okay?"

"I'm fine," I said to her. "In fact I'm beginning to feel like myself again."

"I'm so glad. Dad's in his office. Let me put him on the line."

"Jesse," said the familiar voice that still could make me feel weak. "I was going to call you." In the background I heard Argus bark. "Argus knows it's you on the phone."

"That's because he heard you say my name," I laughed. "I miss you guys."

"We miss you, too."

"When are you coming?" I asked.

"We just got a missing person's case. It's a child. I've got my son-in-law working on it. But he's going to need my help." Tim's son-in-law, Derek Cooper, was chief of police; a position Tim held until retirement.

"Any leads?" I asked.

"Several," Tim said, "but I could use that Voodoo that you do so well."

"Very funny," I said. "Intuition is not Voodoo."

"It is the way you do it. Besides intuition isn't really a good word for what you and Monica come up with."

"Ending a sentence with a preposition? Have I taught you nothing?"

"I know. A preposition is a bad thing to end a sentence with," admitted Tim in a mocking tone. He knows I could give a crap about grammar now that I wasn't in the classroom.

"Anyway, the weather here is lovely, so get here as soon as you are able. Is Hugh back from Montreal?" I asked.

"I'm a little worried. I haven't heard from him in a week. His phone just goes to voice mail."

"That's odd. Have him call me when you do get hold of him."

"You haven't heard from him either?" asked Tim.

"I've been neglectful about keeping in touch with everyone," I admitted.

"Yes, so I've noticed."

"When you come here you'll understand. One day just blends into another and you lose track of time. It's called paradise for a reason. I should let you go," I said reluctantly.

"Love you," he said.

"Love you, too big guy." And I ended the call. I think it was a good sign that I was beginning to miss the people in my life and wasn't so focused on my health.

Hanauma Bay is known for its clear water and variety of sea life. It's a state park and we were required to watch a short introductory film. After the film Travis headed to the water, but I took a short introductory lesson in snorkeling, having never done it before. I was self conscious at first about being in just swim trunks in public, but looking around at all the tourists I began to feel better. So far I had avoided the middle age spread. Then I remembered I was only middle aged if the human life span was one hundred-twenty years long. It wasn't.

My first sight of Travis Chan shirtless made me do a double take. Both Tim and Hugh have great bodies, but Travis looked like a body builder. I had to put my mask on and swim away to keep from being distracted.

The sights underwater were amazing, and I enjoyed the feeling of swimming along with my face in the water. I wondered why it had taken me so long to discover snorkeling, and then I remembered that I live in Maine, The only way you could get me into the cold Atlantic water would be with a wet suit, and then I would probably suffer a hydrothermal reaction.

At some point I knew I had to get out of the water. I was using muscles I didn't know I had, and I was beginning to tire out. I headed out of the water and found the beach blanket that Travis had brought along and stretched out. I must have fallen asleep because the next thing I knew Travis was shaking me awake.

"We better get you out of the sun," he said as he began to pack up. "Let's go to my place for a drink."

"Fine with me," I replied. "I could use a drink."

He put extra towels on the seats to protect them from our wet swim wear, though they were beginning to dry. Once again as we drove along I saw sights I hadn't seen before. A little later we rolled into his driveway and headed into his house.

"A glass of wine?" he asked.

"That would be most welcome," I responded. He went into his kitchen and returned with two glasses of wine.

"Cheers!" he said.

"Cheers," I echoed.

"Now," he said moving closer to me, "let's get you out of those wet clothes."

"I…" I started to say and then, well…

"**H**ow was your day?" I asked Jay once I got back to the condo.

"It was a long tour. I think tomorrow I'm just going to relax. In two days I have to get back on the plane. How was your day?"

"I went snorkeling," I answered.

"And I bet it was with that hunky detective Chan."

"Yes, I don't know about hunky, though." Liar, Liar I thought to myself as I pictured the shirtless detective.

Jay looked at me and narrowed his eyes. "Don't forget," he reminded me, "that you are not the only psychic in the family."

"Lovely weather, don't you think?" I said changing the subject.

"Nice try," he responded. "Now tell me about your day."

Chapter 13

The index cards were on the table. Jay and I had spent the evening filling out the events and details of the Takamoura case. Next we looked into the purchase of the classic VW van. It was more expensive than Bill Takamoura could afford working in a surf shop. Interviewing the sister we learned that she was unaware of the van purchase. The sister said that the last time she saw him he was upbeat and talked about coming into money. Jay dutifully filled out the card as we went along.

"Then," I continued as Jay wrote, "we interview his boss, Donny Smith, at the surf shop. Something about him bothered me."

"Shall I write that part down?" asked Jay.

"Yes, it will remind me to ask Travis if he looked into Smith's background. Smith gave us the name of the guy who sold the van to Bill."

"What was the name?" Jay asked as he paused in his writing.

"Peter Thompson. He told us that Takamoura paid twenty-five thousand dollars in cash for the van."

"That's a lot of cash," said Jay who lives on a teacher's salary.

"Travis and I went to Takamoura's apartment and again it was very expensive and not something he could afford on his surf shop pay. It was there that we discovered the black book that led us to believe that he was running a prostitution business."

"That's going to take up two note cards," said Jay who seemed shocked at the findings.

The phone rang and I saw the caller ID and sighed. I answered it, and then passed the phone to Jay.

"It's your grandmother," I said as he took the phone. He rolled his eyes.

As he spoke his expression changed. When he hung up he said, "She seems more normal. What happened? She doesn't seem as crazy."

I explained about the operation that helped open up the blood flow to her brain, "But," I said, "make no mistake, the woman is still crazy."

"Was she always like that?"

"My parents were never Ozzie and Harriet," I said.

"Who?"

"Never mind."

I was getting worried. I hadn't heard from Hugh Cartier in two weeks and apparently neither had Tim. Hugh and I met in Montreal when he was investigating the murder of my instructor at the culinary school. He and I had struck up a friendship and had moved in with Tim and me when he suffered a heart attack. He had returned to Montreal to take care of some business and we hadn't heard from him since.

One of his sons had moved to Ontario and I gave him a call. He was surprised that his father had returned to Montreal, and no, he hadn't heard from him in a few weeks. I picked up the phone and called the Bath Police Department and was put through to Derek Cooper.

"Jesse," said Derek, "good to hear from you. How's Hawaii?"

"Hawaii," I replied, "is great. But I have something for you to check out." I explained about not hearing from Hugh for a couple of weeks. "And I need you to see what you can find."

"I suppose Jessica and I could go up to Montreal for a couple of days,' he offered.

"Ask Tim for the condo keys. It might be a little musty because neither Tim nor I have been there for a few months."

"Don't worry about that. I could use a few days off so we'll be happy to go up there."

"Great, keep me informed."

"I will," he replied. "When are you coming home?"

"I guess when I begin to feel like myself again."

"We all miss you here."

"I think you all would be relieved to be rid of the cranky old man."

"Not at all," he said. "Now I need to go deal with the world of crime."

"Okay, thanks Derek," I said as I ended the call.

Johnny Chapman was tending the bar as I entered the Torch Light. "The usual?" he asked me as I sat down at the bar.

"Whiskey sour. I need something strong." He mixed the drink and added the fruit.

"What's going on?" he asked concerned as he passed me the drink.

"I'm working on an unsolved murder, I have a friend who seems to be missing, and my head doesn't seem to be working well."

"Is that all?" he laughed. "How can I help?"

"You can bring me another one of these," I said holding up my empty glass.

"Easy there," he said.

"Believe it or not, I'm a three drinks a week guy, and mostly wine. Just another example of my being not myself."

"When does your son go back home?" he asked avoiding my lament.

"Saturday morning."

"Let's throw him a party tomorrow night then," offered Johnny. "I know a great little restaurant, and we'll get Travis to come and the four of us can have a nice dinner."

"That would be great," I said feeling better for some reason.

Johnny drove into the heart of Honolulu and I was completely lost. Travis and Jay were in the back seat. We pulled up into a parking area and Johnny turned his keys over to a valet as we stepped out of the car.

"Fancy," said Jay as he looked at the building. It was ornate in an Asian style, and much more tastefully decorated than Wong Ho's Restaurant back home. Along the walls were what I guessed were actual artifacts from China's past. We were taken to a back room that was filled with little dining area separated by curtains. Most of the other patrons, I noticed, were locals.

"Travis was the one who first took me here," said Johnny.

"Some distant relatives own this," said Travis.

"If the food is as good as the atmosphere," I remarked looking around, "then we are in for a good meal."

"Just don't confuse the food here with the Chinese-American stuff back home. This is authentic grub," said Travis.

"Well," said my son, "I think I'd like an authentic drink. It will be a long flight back home."

Chapter 14

Jay caught the hotel shuttle to the airport in the morning. It had been a good visit, but it had tired me out. I worried that I was too slow gaining back my stamina. I was due to have my blood checked out, and my doctor had given me the name of a clinic in Honolulu.

I had been stuck with so many needles and IVs during the last year, that I hardly felt the needle as the nurse drew my blood. They sent me back to the waiting room while the lab checked out my blood.

"Mr. Ashworth," said the nurse as she came out to get me, "the doctor will see you now." I was holding my breath. What if the blood count was off and the chemo didn't work. Then I realized that I'd have periodic blood tests for the rest of my life.

"How are you feeling?" the doctor asked me.

"I was going to ask you the same question," I said trying to lighten the mood. "Actually I seem to tire easily still."

"Well, your white count is normal. You are slightly anemic which would explain your fatigue. That will straighten out in time. Eat a balanced diet and get plenty of rest."

I left the clinic feeling much lighter, and headed over to the Torch Light for a celebratory drink.

I woke up after a restless nap and realized I needed to get something accomplished on the Takamoura case. I needed to clear my head and shake out the cobwebs so I headed to the beach, took off my sandals, and walked along the sand letting the water lap at my feet. As I cleared my head various images popped into my inner vision. I've always found it hard to distinguish intuition from imagination, so while I take these impressions seriously, I find it wise to pay attention, but not place too much trust in them.

Once again I was seeing the image of a pineapple, just as Monica had the last time I talked to her. I wished she were here. So far Jay was the only one who had flown out here to see me. Everyone else said they were planning to fly in, but no one had made definite plans. I was worried about Hugh and hadn't heard anything from Derek in his search. Just as I was heading back from my walk I received a message from Travis telling me he would be at the condo in an hour.

I headed back to the condo, hopped in the shower, and put on at pair of shorts and a new shirt I had picked up yesterday. As soon as I dressed the doorman buzzed me to tell me detective Chan was on his way up.

"Hey, Jesse," he said as he came through the door. "You've finally got some color."

"Well," I responded, "I am beginning to feel better," I really don't like talking about my health so I changed the subject. "Anything new on the Takamoura case?"

"That's why I'm here. Have you run across any new leads?"

"Honestly, I've got nothing. You?"

"I just got a report on the owner of the surf shop."

"Donny Smith? What did you find out?"

"Not much. Never been in trouble as far as we know. He's from the Midwest, in his fifties, and came over here to become a surfer. He was a good surfer, but never managed to be competitive, so he opened a surf shop."

"How did he make his money?" I asked. "Surfing doesn't pay."

"He held odd jobs here and there."

"Odd jobs wouldn't pay enough to begin a surf shop," I said.

"His family had money."

"That makes sense."

"So you have nothing?" asked Travis.

"Well, here goes." I told him about how Monica and I were trained by our Spiritualists grandparents. I also told him about how we both saw the vision of a pineapple. "I know it sounds crazy but…"

"This is Hawaii," he responded. "We have a long history of belief in the world of spirits. So, yes, I believe you. I'm not sure how a pineapple fits into the case."

"Me either yet," I said.

"Want to come over tonight? I'm cooking one of my spam specialties."

"Only if you share some of your recipes. I do write cookbooks you know," I said.

"No problem. I'll share my recipes and a few other things too," he said with a wicked smile.

I was alone on the beach. That is I was alone on the beach with three hundred other souls who were alone on the beach with me. I was walking along when my phone started to vibrate. I looked at the caller ID.

"Where the hell have you been?" Hugh must have thought I sounded angry because he started on the defensive.

"I've been in northern Quebec visiting my elderly aunt. There's no cell service up there."

"No post office either? You could have written."

"I wasn't expecting to stay that long. Now if you let me get in a word without you getting crazy, I'd like to know how you are feeling."

I relaxed. "I'm getting a little bit better every day. My blood work came back normal."

"That's good news," he said.

"Sorry if I sounded a little gruff. I was worried about you."

"You're the first one I called. Who is there with you?" he asked."

"No one. It seems everyone has something to finish up. Where are you? Derek and Jessica are in Montreal looking for you."

"You sent them up here to look for me?"

"It was an excuse to get them to take a vacation. They're at the condo," I told him.

"I'll go over and let them know I'm here."

"And you need to call Tim and let him know you're safe."

"He's my next call," he said.

"When are you coming out here?" I asked.

"As soon as I can get a cheap flight. Can't wait to see you."

"Lot's going on here. I'll tell you all about it when you get here."

"Intriguing. I'll sign off now. Can't wait to see you."

"Back at you," I said and we ended the call. Hugh Cartier, tall and with those Irish good looks and French charm, and built for looks. Like Tim, he is absolutely easy on the eyes.

I passed some freak passing out religious pamphlets. "Have you been washed in the blood of the lamb?" he asked as he passed me the leaflet.

"No, but I did take a shower this morning," I said as I kept walking.

Chapter 15

When I arrived at Travis's house both Johnny Chapman and Lisa Takamoura were already there. I didn't know they were coming. I was relieved not to be alone with Travis. After all life was complicated enough.

"I thought," said Travis as I walked into the house, "that if the four of us put our heads together we might come up with something."

"Not a bad idea," I said.

"Let's have dinner first before we talk about murder," said Travis. "I've made Hawaiian pulled chicken sandwiches and fries."

"Sounds interesting," I said. I wondered what made pulled chicken Hawaiian.

"We'll start with Mai Tais or if you prefer beer," offered Travis.

Dinner was interesting. The three of them discussed Hawaiian history, which I knew little about. What I found interesting was how life on the island changed during World War II.

After dinner Travis got down to business. "Lisa, tell us about your brother during the last year. Anything that might help us."

"My brother and I were close, and as I've said before we went to church on Sundays together and out to brunch, and a few times a week he would come over for dinner. He kept a room at the house but rarely used it."

"I always thought you two were close," said Johnny.

"As far as I knew," she continued, "he worked at the surf shop and did odd jobs to get his money."

"How did you think he afforded the expensive apartment?" I asked.

"We were left some money when our parents passed on. I had no idea about his running a.." she hesitated looking for the right word. "…business."

"And you said," Travis continued the question, "that he told you he was coming into some money?"

"He said he was working on something that would pay off," she answered.

"What about your friendship with Takamoura?" Travis asked Johnny.

"I knew him mostly from the bar. He came in almost every day. We had gone surfing together a few times."

"Did he ever hit on the other customers?" I asked.

"Not really," Johnny said. "Billy would talk to the other patrons, but I never noticed anything beyond that. I knew he liked to be admired by the men."

"Isn't that an unusual behavior?" I asked and realized this was the third time I had asked. Duh!

"You would be surprised," said Johnny. "Straight men come into the bar all the time. I think they just want to reassure themselves that they are attractive."

"Interesting," I said. "And he told you he was going to come into some money?"

"He did," answered Johnny. "But I thought it was just talk."

"Have either of you ever seen this before?" Travis asked Lisa and Johnny as he produced the little black book. Neither of them had seen it before they claimed.

"It's in code. We don't know what the code is," he continued. "Plus we have a thumb drive that replicates the material, but without the code it's useless.

The voice in my head was shouting "alphabet." I took the black book from Travis and went off to the kitchen by myself and got strange looks from everyone. I focused on the page and then closed my eyes and meditated. In my mind the letters began to shift around until I got the answer to the code. I opened my eyes and began to decode the first sentence. It worked. I rejoined the others in the living room and threw the book down on the coffee table.

"Got it," I said.

"Got what?" asked Travis.

"The code," I explained. "It's a simple letter shift. Case in point, the first letter of the sentence is a one letter shift up the alphabet. For instance in the letter shift B become C. Then the second letter is a shift down the alphabet, so B becomes A. So every letter alternates from a shift up and then a shift down." They looked at me like I had just discovered the cure for dementia. Or maybe they thought I was suffering dementia. Either way I liked the attention.

"How did you figure that out?" asked Travis. "I've been trying to figure it out since we found it."

"It's because I'm a freaking genius," I said. Might as well blow my own horn. No one else will.

"Sure, that's it," said Travis rolling his eyes.

"I saw that," I responded.

"Coffee and dessert?" asked Travis. "I know now I'll be up all night trying to decode this."

We had coffee and pineapple upside-down cake, and then we left Travis alone to work on the black book.

When I got back to the condo the doorman gave me a note that had been left on my door. It was from Rhonda. She had flown into Honolulu and was staying at the Tower Hotel. It was late and I knew she would be asleep with jet lag. I called the hotel and left a message for her to meet me for breakfast, and that she should call me when she wakes up.

I was on my third bathroom trip of the night and had just crawled back into bed when the phone rang. "What's with all this *aloha* crap," said a voice on the other end of the phone.

"*Aloha*, Rhonda," I said just to be annoying. "What the hell time is it?"

"It's five o'clock in the morning and I'm starving."

"Honey, you could go a month without starving."

"Are you calling me fat, you little toad," she sputtered.

"Well, you know, if the dress doesn't fit."

"Anyway, why don't you get your ass out of bed and buy a girl breakfast."

"Okay, I just need to hop in the shower and do my beauty routine."

"That would take a decade for the beauty part and we may not have that much time left. You are getting on, you know."

"I'm still five years younger than you," I reminded her. "I'm hanging up now. I'll be over shortly."

The Tower Hotel was about five blocks from the condo, and it was a fine morning for a walk. It was now a little after six and the real Hawaiians were heading to work while the tourists slept. It was noisy with all the early morning deliveries to the hotels.

Rhonda was waiting for me in the hotel's lobby, and I braced myself for her unusual clothing choices. Rhonda collects and wears vintage clothing and you never know what decade she will be wearing. To my surprise she was wearing almost normal clothing. Tan shorts and a golfing blouse, and sensible shoes.

"What's with the lesbian look?" I asked as we hugged.

"Stereotyping? Good to see you, too," she said. "I need to go clothes shopping. I already have the name of a few vintage clothing stores the concierge gave me."

"Awesome," I said as I rolled my eyes.

"Enough of your bitchiness," she said. "Let's get some food."

"There's a little place around the corner that serves breakfast. It's good to see you," I said. "I've missed you."

"I've missed you, too," she said. We were shown to a table with a nice water view and given menus. "Now, tell me what you have been up to."

Chapter 16

Rhonda packed away a huge breakfast as I explained about the Takamoura case. To her credit she didn't ask me how I was feeling. I was tired of having to explain that I felt well, but still tired easily. I wanted to forget the whole of last year.

"Did your six sense give you any clues about the killer?" she asked. Rhonda was a true believer, and I never had to explain myself to her.

"I had a flash image of a pineapple. Monica said she had the same image in her mind."

"Well, there you go," said Rhonda. "What more do you need?"

"This is Hawaii," I responded. "There are acres and acres of pineapples."

"You'll figure it out." I wish I was as confident as she was.

"So what's up with Jackson?" I asked to change the subject.

"He says he's too busy to take time off and fly out here, but I know that he just doesn't want to fly."

"I can't blame him. I had to take a week to get here,"

"You're a pussy I flew out here with no problem."

"Yes, but you are bat-shit crazy."

"Nice talk. You kiss your boyfriends with that mouth?"

"Boyfriends?"

"How long have I known you?" she asked knowing full well what the answer was."

"Thirty-five years or so," I admitted. "Now where are these vintage clothing stores you want to visit?"

By the end of the morning Rhonda had a whole new wardrobe, and I had sore feet from walking. Rhonda, however, seemed tireless. But of course that's because she loved shopping. "What are you going to do with this?" I asked pointing to a woman's military uniform from the Second World War.

"Costume party."

"The last costume party you came as Jackie Kennedy with the bloody pink suit."

"It made a statement," she said defensively.

"Yes, a statement of poor taste." At this she gave me a rude finger gesture.

I suggested that she take a nap for jet lag, and I went off to see what I could dig up about Bill Takamoura. I went back to the condo to change when Travis Chan called me. "We've decoded Takamoura's black book thanks to you."

"You would have figured it out eventually," I said. "It really was a simple code."

"It's not really one of my talents. Meet me at the Torch Light in half an hour."

"Okay. See you there," and I ended the call.

Travis Chan arrived at the Torch Light about ten minutes after I got there. He was dressed in a white shirt with a red tie which really set off his tan good looks. I wasn't the only one who noticed and heads swiveled.

After an initial greeting Travis took on a serious look. "Jesse, I think you need to drop the investigation and let the police handle it."

"And why is that?" I asked.

"Apparently someone in the department learned I was working with you. The higher-ups weren't happy about me working with a private detective."

"So you want me to drop the case?" I asked.

"Yes, I think it would be for the best."

"Not going to happen, Travis. I don't give up."

"I thought you would say that," he said as he reached into his pocket for a pack of folded sheets and put them on the table.

"What's that?" I asked unfolding the papers.

"I should go. Keep me updated if you find out anything," and he got up and headed out the door.

"What was all that about?" asked Johnny as he came over.

"I have no idea," I replied. Then I began reading the material Travis passed me. "Whoa," I said aloud. It was the decoded information of Takamoura's black book.

I decided to take a nap before meeting Rhonda for dinner later. I was dreaming strange dreams. I was in a pineapple field and running after a truck that I couldn't catch. Running and running and I finally woke up and the word 'truck' stuck in my head. I picked up the phone and called Monica.

"Truck," I said as Monica answered.

"Jesse? What are you talking about?"

"I had a dream that I was in a pineapple field chasing a truck I could not catch."

"Okay," she said. "Let me process this and I'll call you right back."

I went out to the kitchen and made myself a cup of coffee. I had just sat down when Monica called me back. "I think you are on to something," she said. "I meditated and the image of a truck came to me. You find the truck and you'll find the killer."

"Gee, finding a truck in Hawaii should be easy," I said with a tone of sarcasm. "There probably aren't more than a few thousand trucks here."

"You'll know it when you see it," she said with confidence.

"I wish I was as sure as you," I sighed.

"Relax," she said, "and go along for the ride."

"Sure thing," I agreed and we ended the call.

As I sat back on the lanai and read through the list of names from the black book nothing really seemed to stick out. I was confident that many of the names were tourist to Oahu who would be long gone, but there were several names that had a number after them. Somehow I divined that the numbers represented repeat customers. The list of sex workers consisted of mostly female names, but interestingly there were a few male names as well. At the end of the papers Travis gave me was photocopies of the original pages of the black book.

As an English teacher I was used to deciphering hand writing, so as I looked at the handwriting a thought struck me, and I knew what my next move would be.

Chapter 17

Lisa Takamoura sat back and looked at the photocopies I had brought along. Johnny Chapman had offered to drive me to her house on the north coast, and we had a pleasant talk on the way to Lisa's house.

"Is this your brother's handwriting?" I asked.

"No, clearly it isn't. What does this mean?"

"It means," I replied, "that we now have a motive for your brother's murder. He was not running a prostitution ring. He most likely stole this book from someone and was blackmailing someone on the list, or he was blackmailing the ring leader."

"So what is the significance?" she asked.

"Well, let's take a look at the case so far," I began. "Your brother was murdered either in the van or was placed in the van. The van was parked near Kapiolani Park. Why? Maybe it was to send a message to others, or maybe just for revenge. We know your brother was living beyond his means. There are two scenarios: one is that he was part of the ring, or he got hold of the black book and was blackmailing someone. Either way someone was paying him and needed to get rid of him."

"Do you think," asked Johnny, "that Bill was able to decode the book?"

"Probably not," I answered, "but who ever owned the black book wouldn't know that."

"So what do you do next?" asked Lisa.

"I need to share this information with the police. I'll need to think about my next move."

"Do you need more money?" she asked.

"Right now your retainer has covered my expenses and time. I think we can solve the case in a few days."

"You do?" asked Johnny.

"It's a feeling I have," I answered and left it at that.

When I got back to the condo I called Travis, and he agreed to meet me at the Torch Light later. I walked over to the Tower Hotel where I picked up Rhonda to take her for dinner.

"What type of food do you want to try?" I asked her.

"Cake!" she said. "I want cake!" Rhonda's love of cake could be classified as a mental disorder.

"I mean before dessert."

"I'm not sure," she admitted.

"Well, there's a buffet restaurant a few blocks from here. That will let you try different dishes. Some of the Hawaiian food is really good," I said.

"Some?"

"Well," I said to her, "I can eat most anything, but you are more fussy than I."

"Glad to see your grammar hasn't slipped, but I'm not fussy."

"To hell you're not," and I started to laugh. Laughing felt good.

"And is there a dessert buffet?"

"Of course," I responded.

"Let's go," she said as she pinned a pillbox hat on her head, which I noticed matched her 1960s outfit. "I'm starving."

Rhonda and I sat in a corner of the Torch Light. She was facing the door. "I'll bet that's your cop coming in now," she said.

I turned to see Travis Chan enter the bar. "How did you know?"

"I know you. Mature, good looking, broad shoulders, and flat stomach," she recited. "I know your type."

"You think so?" I asked. I knew what she was going to say.

"Just like you are drawn to yellow painted houses, you are drawn to powerfully built men." Rhonda had once pointed out that every house I liked was yellow.

"Travis, this is my friend Rhonda Shepard," I introduced the two.

"I'm Jesse's fag hag," she said as she shook his hand.

"I think that's an outdated phrase," I said.

"You're outdated," she flung back at me.

"Nice to meet you, Rhonda. Has Jesse told you what we are up to?"

"Not everything," she said looking at him up and down."I'm sure he's left out a few of the more intimate events. But if you mean the murder, yes he has." Travis blushed. We were saved from any more awkwardness by Johnny who came over and sat with us.

"Gee, Jesse," said Rhonda not ready to give up her needling me. "Two good looking men. You must be in heaven."

"Anyway," I said ignoring the jab, "there's been a development in the Takamoura case."

"I'm listening," said Travis.

"I visited the sister and had her look at the photocopies you gave me. She claims that the handwriting is not his."

"So that means he's not involved in the prostitution ring," said Johnny.

"Not necessarily," I replied. "It means that the book isn't his. He could still be involved."

"Blackmail?" asked Travis as he processed the information.

"That's what I was thinking," I said. "Remember, he was telling people that he was coming into some money."

"Makes sense," added Johnny. He motioned over one of the waiters. "Drinks are on me. What will you have?"

We gave the waiter our orders and he brought over a bowl of nuts. "The lab," continued Travis, "checked the book for fingerprints, but the only fingerprints they found belonged to Takamoura."

"So where do we go from here?" I asked.

"I think," Travis turned to me, "that we should resume working together."

"What about your bosses at the department?" I asked.

'I'm going to insist that we work with you. Actually they've checked your background and are impressed with your success rate."

"Okay," I agreed.

"Now," said Travis, "let's relax."

"Ronda and I are planning on going to the buffet restaurant if you two would like to join us."

"I'm in," said Travis.

"Me, too," said Johnny.

Chapter 18

The trouble with Paradise is that one day melts into another and if you are not careful you lose track of the days. I wasn't careful. I rented a car for a few days and Rhonda and I went sightseeing. She wanted to see Pearl Harbor and the Arizona, the Valley of the Temples, and of course the circle tour of the island. Several days had slipped away with good food and beautiful scenery, and I had done nothing on the Takamoura case.

Even though I wasn't actively working the case, the little voices in my head were chatting away. You know that voice. The one that keeps up a running comment on everything and the one that makes it difficult to meditate because it won't shut the hell up. At any rate my mind was working in the background and I came up with an idea.

Rhonda and I went to the Torch Light for after dinner drinks, and I asked Johnny to join us. "What's up?" he asked.

"Looking over the list of workers in the black book, I was wondering if you would recognize any of the names. Even though they seem to be nicknames I thought you might recognize who they belong to." I was going to say "to whom the names belong," but I didn't want to sound too much like an English teacher.

"What makes you think I would know them?" he asked.

"Bill Takamoura, supposedly straight, hung out here. Why? Because maybe one or more of the sex workers hang out here."

"I'll take a look," he agreed looking skeptical. I passed him a list of the prostitutes with the male names highlighted in green. His finger went down the list and then stopped. "This one, I've seen this guy they call Boomer. He comes in here all the time."

"Is he here now?" I asked. Johnny looked around and shook his head. "I don't see him. He only comes in two or three times a week."

"Thanks," I said as Johnny got up to return to the bar.

"You have an exciting job," remarked Rhonda shaking her head. "Are you sure you don't want to come back and work for me at Erebus?"

"Handling internet sales for a gift shop is a real snooze," I replied. "No, thank you."

"Spoil sport," she said. While we were trading jabs I saw a guy walk into a bar who looked familiar, but it took me a few moments to place him. I grabbed my baseball cap and put it on and lowered the visor to hide my face a bit.

"What are you doing?" she asked.

"The guy who just walked in is the guy that sold Takamoura the red van. His name is Peter Thompson."

"So?" she asked.

"So, it sometimes helps to follow any leads that happen to fall in my path. Anyone that has anything to do with Bill Takamoura deserves a closer look." Trying to both keep my head down and watch Thompson was a challenge. Finally he settled down to a table with his back to me and I could observe what he was doing.

"Are you having one of your spells?" she asked looking heavenward.

"Spells?"

"You know, when you go all Twilight Zone on us."

"Intuition," I said, "has nothing to do with the Twilight Zone you know. Everyone has it."

"Not like you and your family they don't."

As I watched, a good looking young man came into the bar and sat down with Thompson. Johnny rushed over and whispered in my ear. "That's Boomer," he said.

"Well," I said more to myself than to Rhonda and Johnny, "things just got interesting." Johnny went back to the bar, but kept his eyes on Boomer. I saw money change hands and Peter Thompson got up and left.

"What are you going to do?" asked Rhonda as I started to get up out of my chair.

"Watch this," I said as I headed over to Boomer's table. "Hello," I said to him. He looked up and smiled.

"Have a seat," he said to me. "They call me Boomer."

"I'm Jesse. You come here often?" If that wasn't a classic pick up line, I don't know what is."

"Yes," he responded, "It's a good place to meet men. Are you looking for company?"

"That would be nice."

"Are you generous?" he asked. I hadn't heard the term before, but I knew he was asking me if I was willing to pay for, as he put it, 'company.'

"Yes, I am," I said as I reached into my pocket and threw my private investigator license on the table. He got up to leave. "Sit down," I said. "You can talk to me or you can talk to the police." He sat back down and looked frightened.

"First of all, I could care less about your business. All I want from you is some information. Tell me what I want to know and the police won't need to know anything about your occupation."

"What do you want?"

"Tell me about Peter Thompson," I said.

"What do you mean?" he asked.

"Don't play dumb with me or I'll make a call to my friend Homicide Detective Chan."

"Homicide?" he turned pale and began to shake.

"Never mind that, is Peter Thompson running a prostitution ring?"

"He calls it a dating service," said Boomer.

"I'll take that as a yes. What part of the operation did Bill Takamoura play in the business?"

"I don't think he knew anything about the business. As far as I know Takamoura was just his surfing buddy."

"I see." In the back of my mind some pieces fell into place, but I didn't have time at the moment to examine the puzzle. I did realize that Johnny had called Travis Chan when he saw me head over to Boomer's table, because just then Travis walked through the door, headed over to the table and sat down. "This is Detective Chan," I said. 'And this young man is Boomer."

"Well, Boomer," said Travis, "let's start with your real name."

"My real name is Theodore Branson, but everyone calls me Boomer."

"I think you better tell Detective Chan what you told me," I said. Boomer repeated his story and Travis told him that if he cooperated with the investigation that he wouldn't be prosecuted for his part in the 'dating' business.

Chapter 19

Rhonda Shepard was dressed in a Japanese robe when she opened her hotel door. It looked expensive, and I knew she bought it at one of the vintage clothing stores she had dragged me to. She had started packing for the trip back home and there were two suitcases open on the floor with clothing already folded up in them.

"Are you going out for breakfast in that outfit?" I asked.

"And good morning to you, too. And speaking of outfits since when do you wear shorts and sandals?" You look like a Tommy Bahama model, except sort of faded."

"Faded?"

"Anyway, I thought we would have room service breakfast brought up."

"Not a bad idea," I agreed and sat down in one of the comfy chairs. She passed me a room service menu and I chose a plate of eggs and sausage. "Are you sure you don't want to stay here longer?"

"As much as I like it here, it's time for me to go back. What about you?" she asked. "It's almost spring. When are you going back?"

"As soon as the last snow storm melts away," I responded. "And I need to finish the Takamoura case."

"How is that going?"

"Well, I have a theory about the murder, but no solid evidence. Without evidence, Travis can't make an arrest. And I still have pieces of the puzzle that don't fit."

"What pieces?" she asked. Rhonda of course knows about my intuition, and has seen me use it.

"I had a... I guess you could call it a vision. I saw a pineapple and a truck. Monica says I'm on the right track."

"So who did it?" she asked.

"Peter Thompson," I said. "He ran the prostitution ring. I think Bill Takamoura found the black book and was blackmailing him."

"But you can't prove it?" she asked.

I was about to explain more when breakfast arrived. "What time does the van come to take you to the airport?"

"They'll be here in about an hour, so eat up."

I hugged Rhonda good bye and waved to her as the van took off for the airport. I didn't envy her long ride and the jet lag she was going to experience. I was alone once more, and though I had made new friends on the island, I was beginning to feel homesick. I decided then and there that as soon as I finished the case for Lisa Takamoura, I would head for home.

My phone went off as I was walking back to the condo. I looked at the blue sky and the gentle trade winds that moved the palm leaves, and thought to myself this really was paradise. At least compared to the long, cold Maine winters.

"It's Travis," said the voice on the other end. "I'm working late today, but you want to meet me around seven tonight for a drink at the Torch Light?"

"Yes, that sounds great. See you there." I ended the call and headed toward the beach. If Peter Thompson was the murderer, I needed to prove it. It was time to head back to the surf shop and see if Donny Smith remembers anything Takamoura might have said about Peter Thompson.

Johnny Chapman had offered to take me on a tour of some out of the way places on the island on his day off. It was a Tuesday and I knew he would be home so I gave him a call.

"Jesse, good to hear from you," he said when he answered.

"I was wondering if that offer of the island tour was still good."

"Today would be a great day to do that," he said. "I've got the day off and nothing better to do."

"I was wondering if we could stop at the surf shop where Takamoura worked. I have a few questions for Donny Smith."

"That shouldn't be a problem. We'll be heading out that way. I'll pick you up in an hour."

"I'll be ready," I said and headed back to the condo to pick up my camera.

No matter how many times I circle the island, there are always new things to see. I wanted to see as much as possible and take enough photos to remind me of the beauty and magic of Hawaii. I had no idea if or when I'd ever get back here. The surf shop was the last stop.

When Smith saw me enter the shop he looked up and asked me if there were any new developments in the case. "Nothing substantial," I said. It's my policy to not say much until a case is actually solved. "I just have a question for you. Did you ever see Thompson and Takamoura together?"

"Several times."

"How about the days before Takamoura was killed?"

"Actually," said Smith, "I think Thompson's car was in the shop. Bill drove Thompson to the auto shop."

"In the red van?" I asked.

"Yes, in the red van."

Just then Smith's cell phone went off and he answered it. My eyes were drawn to the phone because it was a large size that I knew was expensive. I could never bring myself to pay for any phone that cost more than two hundred dollars. After all don't they all do the same thing?

I waved to Smith who was still on the phone and headed out the door. On a hunch I walked around to the back of the shop, and then I saw something that made all the pieces fall into place, and I knew who killed Takamoura.

The Torch Light was full and overflowing when I entered to meet Travis. "What's the occasion?" I asked Johnny when he took me to a table and sat down with me.

"It's the first day of spring," he said. "A day of celebration."

"Spring? How can you tell?"

"True, it's not like home where we have seasons, but here it's more of a Pagan celebration of the spring equinox."

Travis entered and Johnny waved him over to the table where we were seated. "I should get back to the bar since we are so busy," said Johnny as he got up to leave.

"I think we are close to an arrest in the Takamoura case," said Travis.

"You mean Peter Thompson?"

"Yes, we just need to find the final link."

"You can arrest him for running a prostitution ring," I said, "but he's not Takamoura's murderer."

"You're kidding, right?" asked Travis.

"Here's how it all went down," I said and then told Travis all that I figured out.

Chapter 20

Detective Travis Chan looked at me as he copied down all that I told him. "This all makes sense," he said to me as we sat at the corner table of the bar. "But…"

"But," I took up his train of thought, "how do we prove it? We need evidence."

"Exactly, no district attorney is going to go for your theory without proof."

"I have an idea," I said as I took a sip of my umbrella drink. "We just need to find the murder weapon."

"That's all?" Travis laughed. "That thing is long gone."

"Think about it," I said referring back to the coroner's report. "He was hit by a broad blunt object."

"Which could be anything," he said rolling his eyes.

"I guess you're right," I said somewhat deflated. I had no idea where to go from here.

"So we really have nothing to go on except your intuition," Travis said. "For the record, I believe you. But we need more."

"Yes, we do," I agreed and then a sudden thought hit me. "What if the murderer wasn't working alone?"

"That makes it even harder to prove."

"But," I insisted, "If there happens to be more than one in on the crime, one of them is liable to be a weak link. For a plea bargain the weak link will sell out the murderer to save himself or herself."

"What do you have in mind?" asked Travis as he finished his drink.

"Confrontation," I explained.

"Interesting," replied Travis. "Let's pick up dinner and head back to my place and plan."

"Let's go," I agreed.

I couldn't remember the last time I had Italian food, so when we picked up dinner to go I ordered lasagna which turned out to be surprisingly good. That reminded me that since I was in Hawaii, I should write down some of the recipes for my next cookbook.

Travis and I didn't discuss the case during dinner, but as soon as we finished and Travis made a pot of Kona coffee we got down to business.

"Do you think," I asked, "that you can get all the major players in one room together?"

"If I make it sound like a request from the police I'm sure they will come. What do you have in mind?"

"I'm going to tell everyone my theory about the murder and see who reacts. The element of surprise should be enough to elicit some type of reaction," I explained.

"That could be risky," said Travis doubtfully.

"It will work," I said sounding more confident than I felt. The little voice in my head assured me it would work, but still…

"Ok," Travis agreed, "let's work out the plan."

I picked up the phone and called my client. "Lisa, it's Jesse. I have an announcement to make about Bill's murder. Could you come to the Torch Light tomorrow morning before it opens, say around nine?" Johnny had offered to host the little get together.

"Did you find the murderer?" she asked sounding excited.

"I'd rather discuss it in person." She assured me that she would be there.

Travis had "requested," that Peter Thompson and Donny Smith attend our little party. Now all I had to do was wait.

Johnny was at the door of the bar greeting our "guests" as they came in. Two plain clothes policemen were behind the bar polishing glasses and looking like they belonged there. Several tables had been pushed together to make seating for our little group. I sat at one end and Detective Travis Chan sat at the other. On my right was Lisa Takamoura, on my left was Donny Smith. Johnny Chapman was beside Travis on his left and Peter Thompson was on his right.

"To begin with," said Travis, "let's clarify our rolls here. First is Lisa, Bill Takamoura's sister. Donny Smith owns the surf shop where Takamoura worked. Peter Thompson was a surfing buddy of Bill's. Jesse Ashworth is a private investigator hired by Lisa Takamoura to find Bill Takamoura's killer. So are we all up to speed now?" Everyone nodded.

"I don't see why we are here," said Donny Smith. "Clearly this was some random act of murder."

"Not true," I said. "Takamoura's murder was planned out in advance. Now I'd like to keep our little meeting as brief as possible so we can get on with the day. So if I may continue without any more interruptions."

"Please go ahead," said Lisa. "I want to hear what Jesse says."

"The solution to the murder was so simple that I should have figured it out days ago. So here's how this all played out." I paused and looked around. Everyone was looking ill at ease. "Bill Takamoura told his sister and Johnny the bar owner that he was going to be coming into some money. One of the first things I noticed was that Bill was living an expensive life-style well beyond what he was making at the surf shop.

"When Lisa hired me, I went to Detective Chan to hopefully read the police report. He agreed that if either of us learned anything of importance that we would share whatever facts we uncover."

"So," Travis took up the story, "I invited Jesse to go along with me to check out Takamoura's apartment. It was clear that someone had gone through the apartment tearing the place up looking for something. This is what we found." Travis threw the black book in the middle of the table.

"The problem," I continued, "was that the book was in code. But it turned out to be a simple code that we were able to decode easily. As it turned out the book was evidence of a prostitution ring. At first we thought that it was Takamoura who was running the ring, but that didn't seem right. What would have been the motive to kill him? So we figured out that Takamoura was a blackmailer. That made a motive more likely."

"So who murdered Bill?" asked Johnny.

"I'm getting to that," I answered. "Stay with me. While most of the sex workers were women, several of them were young men. One of the young men made a habit of hanging out here at the Torch Light. I expect that Johnny knew that solicitation was going on in his bar."

"That's not a crime," said Johnny defensively. "And I had nothing to do with the murder. Bill was my friend."

"As I said," using my best teacher voice, "we can wrap this up sooner if I'm not interrupted. Anyway, it was easy to spot one of the workers who gave up the name of the ring leader."

"I don't have to stay here and listen to these lies," said Peter Thompson as he attempted to get up.

"You realize," I said to him, "that you just self-identified as the ring leader. It was you who ran the prostitution ring. So we thought it was you who most likely was being blackmailed, but then I figured out that while you ran the ring, there was someone else who was the actual head of the prostitution ring.

"I kept seeing the image of a pineapple, and that bothered me. When I went back and looked at the copies of the black book, I saw that someone had sketched the image of a pineapple on one of the pages. I had subconsciously picked up on that image. "Donny. What is the name of your surf shop?"

"Go to hell," he said. "You've got nothing."

"The name of your surf shop is Forbidden Fruit, and your logo is a pineapple. On my last visit to your shop I happened to look behind the building and saw your truck with the logo. So here is what happened," I paused here for effect, plus the fact that the next part of this was conjecture and I hoped I was right.

"Peter's car was in the shop, so Takamoura gave Peter a ride. Peter forgot and left the black book in the van. Takamoura found the book and it was all he needed for blackmail. That book was worth a lot of money.

"Once you discovered that the book was missing you figured out who took it, and you called your boss, who would do anything to get that book back. It was he who murdered Takamoura when he refused to give back the book." The two plainclothes officers had moved behind Donny Smith. "It was you, wasn't it Donny?"

"That's a lie," he said as he tried to get up but was restrained by the two officers.

Travis took over at this point and turned to Peter Thompson. "You are an accessory to murder, but if you cooperate I think the district attorney may broker a plea bargain."

"He did it," said Peter Thompson. "He murdered Takamoura."

"Shut up," screamed Donny Smith as he and Peter Thompson were taken away. Travis then turned to Johnny, "and we need to have a little talk about your clientele."

Chapter 21

It was later that night when the three of us sat in the Torch Light Bar. Johnny had treated us to drinks once again. Travis was telling about how Peter Thompson told the whole story. It was very close to what I had described, except that Thompson claimed he knew nothing about the murder at first, but figured it out quickly.

"It's amazing that you picked up on the pineapple image in the book, "Johnny said to me.

"Except for the fact that there was no pineapple drawing in the book," Travis said.

"Well," I defended myself, "what was I going to say? I was daydreaming and saw a pineapple? I'd have been laughed off of the island."

"So what's next for you?" Johnny asked me.

"I think it's time for me to head home," I told them. "I came here to find myself again. When I first came here I felt lost and adrift. I questioned who I really was. But this place has been magic. I feel like myself again."

"And you are cured?" asked Johnny.

"There really isn't a cure, but there is remission and for now I'm good to go. I would, though, say I'm healed, and both of you were part of that. Johnny, you befriended me when I first arrived, and Travis, you took me along on the murder case, and I was able to forget being sick for the first time in a year. And I love you both for that."

Under the table Travis took my hand and gave it a squeeze. It was going to be hard to leave, but the thought of going home to Tim and my friends was stronger than my desire to stay.

"I think we need to do something with you before you leave," said Travis.

"What's that?"

"You said you've never been to a luau. I don't mean one of those touristy types, but a real luau. My church is having one this weekend. Good food and music. Sorry, but no hula girls. It is a church supper after all."

"I think I'll survive without the hula girls," I said and we all laughed.

The flight was uneventful. I stayed two nights in San Francisco at a hotel near Fishermen's Warf before heading back to Maine. Tim picked me up at the airport in Portland. I was jet lagged so we spent the night in Portland before heading to Bath. I realized how much I missed Tim when I saw his face looking for me in the crowd as I got off the plane.

When we drove up to the house I could hear Argus barking in a shrill bark I hadn't heard before. Viola was dog sitting and when she opened the front door, Argus bounded out and ran for me and jumped in my arms and licked my face.

"He's missed you," said Viola. "We all have."

"Nonsense," I countered. "It was probably better here without me moping around."

"No," said Tim. "No it wasn't."

Going through the front door I was struck with happiness as I looked around. This was home. Home, where I belong. "Get some rest," said Tim. "Everyone is coming over later for dinner, and no you don't have to cook. Wong Ho's Restaurant will be catering the welcome back party."

I felt like my body was still on Hawaiian time, but after an afternoon nap, I was feeling better and looking forward to seeing everyone.

It was later in the afternoon when I woke up from my nap and heard voices. I knew one of the voices belonged to Hugh Cartier. I got up and tried to make myself look presentable. I should explain about Hugh. I met Hugh when I was in Montreal taking a cooking class when the head chef was murdered. Hugh was the homicide detective working the case, and we hit it off. Hugh is tall, dark, and very good looking. It's a tossup who was better looking, Hugh or Tim.

Tim and I own a vacation condo in Montreal, so we got to know Hugh, and when Hugh had a major heart attack, Tim and I suggested he move in with us.

"Look who's back from the dead," said Hugh who came over and hugged me tight.

"I'm not the one who disappeared," I replied. "Everyone knew where I was."

"I didn't mean to make everyone worry, but as you can imagine, northern Quebec province doesn't exactly have internet cafes on every corner, in fact there are no corners."

"What were you doing there?" Tim asked Hugh.

"One of my friends on the police force retired and moved out in the Northern woods. I was up there visiting an elderly aunt when I went to visit him, and wouldn't you know it, there was a report of a missing hiker. He and I went with the RCMP looking for him. The accommodations, when available were rather primitive. And it was still winter up there."

"Did you find the hiker?" I asked him.

"Finally. He had twisted his ankle and took shelter in an old cabin."

There was a knock at the door and the catering crew came in and began setting up in the kitchen. In no time the entire house was filled with the smell of good food.

So far Argus had not let me out of his sight. "Go for a walk?" I asked him and he began to jump around with that pure joy that only dogs can show. "I need some air," I said as I grabbed a jacket and headed out with Argus. Argus and I walked the length of Sagamore Street and then headed back inside.

I changed into dress clothing just before the guests arrived. The first guest was my neighbor Beth White, the local Rabbi; next was my best friend from high school Jason Goulet and my cousin Monica. Viola Vickner, who had gone home to change after dog sitting returned dressed up in what could only be Pagan clothing. She had a black full length dress with signs of the zodiac embroidered on the hem.

Silver haired Jackson Bennett came in next, and I suspected that Rhonda had been in the car waiting for everyone to arrive so she could make an entrance, and she made an entrance for sure. She was dressed in a long evening gown from the 1930s with a matching oversized hat. Covering the dress was a fur stole.

"I hope that's not real fur," I said as I took her stole. "I have some red paint in the garage if it is."

"Lighten up, honey," she replied. "It's fun fur."

"Fun for whom," I shot back. She gave me a semi-obscene finger gesture. "Classy," I said.

"I'm a classy broad," she said. We all rolled our eyes, "I saw that."

"Who wants drinks?" said Tim coming to the rescue.

"Where are the kids?" I asked looking around. The 'kids' were Tim's daughter Jessica and her husband Derek Cooper, and my son Jay and his partner Steven.

"Working," said Tim. "They'll be here for dinner."

After we took our drinks and sat down I said to Tim and Jason, "so tell me about this cases you had that kept you from coming to Hawaii."

"There was the case of the missing child who managed to show up at his grandparents' house. And then the business with missing money. It was," began Jason, "like the case you had in Brunswick awhile back. It was a local business and the owner believed that one of her employees was skimming off some of the profits."

"And you'll never guess who it was," Tim said.

"I'll bet it was a family member," I said as I thought about it.

"Yes, it was the owner's daughter. How did you guess? Of course it wasn't a guess. I should know better that to try to surprise you."

"I had a vision," I said to sound mysterious. Actually I had read about the case when I read one of the back issues of the *Times-Record* online.

Argus began to bark and I knew that the 'kids' had arrived. Jessica came through the door first and ran over and hugged me. "Welcome back, Stepdad!" she said using her nickname for me.

"Yes, welcome back," said the others as they entered.

"It's nice," I said, "to be home with my extended family. I've missed you all." And I tried to keep the tears in check.

Chapter 22

Monday morning rolled around as it always seems to do when one is working. Hugh had gotten up early and made breakfast and Tim had gone off to the office. I made blueberry muffins and packed them up to go in my backpack. I harnessed up Argus and we headed off to the office on foot. The grass seemed to have turned green overnight and the forsythia had broken out its yellow blossoms. Spring had arrived and I was thankful to have missed winter.

This morning I decided to take a detour and walk by the old Huse School on Andrews Road. I spend my early life there, and I heard that it had closed and had now been made into apartments. I remembered the high ceilings and huge windows. It was built during the war in 1942 for the children of shipyard workers, and a newer section was added in 1949 to accommodate the post-war baby boom.

Looking at the building it was evident that a lot of work went into the renovation. I wondered what it would be like to live in an apartment that had been my second grade classroom with Mrs. Young.

Argus began pulling on his leash and snapped me out of my daydreaming. I turned around and headed to the office on Front Street. I stopped briefly at the Erebus gift shop and left muffins for Rhonda and Viola, and then I walked down the street and up the stairs to the office.

Jessica was already at her desk and on the phone. She waved at me as I headed into my office. I fired up my computer and then headed to the break room to unload the muffins and start the coffee.

"Coffee break," I announced and Tim and Jessica joined me in the break room.

"You have an appointment at eleven this morning," Jessica announced as she filled her coffee cup and took a muffin.

"What do they want?" asked Tim.

"Wouldn't say and sounded anxious," she said in a clipped manner.

"If they won't tell you over the phone," I said. "That's never a good sign."

"I guess we'll just have to wait and see," Jessica said as she devoured a muffin.

"And the name?" Tim asked her.

"Chris Drake."

"And he didn't say anything other than he wanted an appointment?" I asked.

"*She* didn't say anything else," Jessica caught me in a sexist moment.

"Oops," I said. "My white privileged male is showing."

Christina Drake appeared somewhere in her late forties and seemed self assured when we met her. She had a firm handshake and got right down to business. She began the session with small talk.

"I think spring has finally come to Bath," she said.

"It has indeed," said Tim cutting short the small talk. "How can we help you?"

"It's my husband," she said and her air of confidence seemed to fade.

"And?" I asked because she hesitated.

"I think he's involved in something. He's been keeping secrets."

"We don't usually get involved in divorce situations," Tim informed her.

"I'm not looking to divorce him. I'm just concerned he might be involved in something illegal."

"You better start at the beginning," I said as I sat back to take notes.

"My husband Daniel is some type of financial adviser. He makes good money some months and others not so much. I work at a doctor's office as a receptionist. It doesn't pay well, but it's a steady income."

"And the name of the doctor?" I asked. She spelled it out for me, and I wrote down the name and address.

"And where does your husband work?" asked Tim.

"He's a freelance agent, so he works in various places."

"Exactly what is it you want us to do?" asked Tim.

"I want you to find him. I've heard you're good at finding missing persons."

"You mean that he disappeared?" I asked. I wanted to ask her why she didn't start with that little piece of information, but it was her dime after all. "When was the last time you saw him?"

"Three days ago. He went off to a meeting in Boston and never returned."

"Did you go to the police?" Tim asked. I could see he was getting exasperated by the slow narrative Christina was giving us.

"No, I'm afraid he's involved in something illegal. I didn't want to get the police involved until I was certain he wasn't in danger."

"If we take the case," I began because I wasn't sure at all that she was forthcoming, "we'll need a photograph, and information about the last conference he attended. And I'm curious as to how you found us?"

"I told my boss about my husband disappearing and she suggested that I contact a private detective. She had heard about you guys from a newspaper article and suggested that I contact you. I have money. Will you take the case?"

Tim looked at me and I shrugged my shoulders. "Yes," said Tim. "We'll take your case. Jessica at the front desk will go over the fee structure with you and have papers for you to sign."

"Thank you. I'll bring in the photo this afternoon."

After she left I turned to Tim, "something about this case is off."

"We don't have any other cases right now, and this sounds interesting if nothing else," said Tim.

I was in the kitchen preparing one pot pasta for dinner as Tim and Hugh came into the kitchen with drinks for the three of us.

"So tell me about this missing husband case," asked Hugh. The three of us sat down at the table with our drinks.

"The husband went to a conference in Boston and disappeared," I said as I sipped my whiskey sour. "The wife hasn't heard from him since. His cell phone goes right to a generic voice mail message."

"How about his car registration?" asked Hugh.

"Apparently he doesn't have his own car," answered Tim

"Maybe he wants to leave her," suggested Hugh.

"We told her that was a possibility and that if we find him, he may not want to come back," I said.

"Or another woman," Hugh continued.

"He is extremely handsome," said Tim. "He's forty-two, full head of hair, tall and a great build."

"You should bring him here," laughed Hugh.

"Two hunky guys are more than I can handle," I laughed.

"You do pretty well with 'handling us'," said Tim making air quotes for emphasis.

"Charming," I said. "Now who's ready to eat?"

Chapter 23

I was slow to wake up and as I began to move, Argus, who had been curled up beside me on the bed, began licking my face. Tim was gone, and I heard voices from the kitchen where I guessed Hugh and Tim were chatting over coffee.

As soon as Tim heard me moving around he went to the cupboard and grabbed the dog dish and filled it with dog food. Argus, who knows all sounds related to food, was off like a shot and was dancing across the floor for his dinner.

"Look who's up?" quipped Hugh as I stumbled into the kitchen. "Coffee?"

"You have to ask?" I grumbled.

"Nope, I guess not." Hugh placed a large cup of coffee in front of me, and then loaded a plate with buckwheat pancakes and bacon.

"That's better," I said after my first sip. "I'll feel human again after a few more sips."

"I hope so," said Tim. "We have a busy day."

"We do?" I asked.

"Missing husband case. You do remember, right?"

"Of course. Handsome tall guy. How could I forget."

"By the way," Tim informed me, "we got an email from Billy Simpson. He and Parker are assigned to a ship that will be doing a transatlantic crossing and then running European cruises for the summer."

"Sounds like a nice life," I commented. Billy Simpson was a high school classmate of ours and Parker Reed and I met years ago when he was a first mate on a Maine windjammer and I was the cook. We shared more than a crew cabin if you get my drift.

"But the work is hard," added Hugh. "They don't have much time off."

"Speaking of time off," I said, "I don't feel like baking this morning, so I'll stop at the coffee shop and pick up some muffins."

"Okay," said Tim heading for the closet to get his jacket, "I'll see you at the office."

"By the way," I said once Tim left, "you're looking mighty fine."

"So are you. Are you feeling better?"

"More and more every day," I answered. "This has done a real number on me. Plus I feel guilty."

"Guilty? Why?"

"Because I was able to leave the clinic and walk away. Others there were not so lucky."

"That shouldn't diminish your story. Think of it this way. Those nurses see terrible things, but how nice when they can send someone on their way."

"Anyway, I am feeling better." I got up and hugged Hugh. "Thanks for being in my life."

Argus was pulling on his leash as we headed out the door and began walking to the office. Just the act of walking the mile to work without tiring out was a gift. I had vowed to walk as much as possible since I walked out of the clinic for the last time.

We passed the house I grew up in and stopped to look at it. The memories came flooding back. My parents had worked hard and saved money and pushed me toward college. I couldn't decide if I missed them, or missed the way they used to be. I had called them last night to check on my mother and she seemed to be doing well.

Brian Stillwater was tending the coffee shop when I got there to buy muffins. "Welcome back, Jesse," He said. Brian has long white hair and follows Native American spiritual ways. As always he was dressed in denim and wearing lots of turquoise jewelry. "How was Hawaii?"

"Magical." I said. "Anyone in need of healing should go there."

"I understand it's a very spiritual place."

"It was for me," I said as I pictured myself walking along the beach and swimming in the water. I ordered a half dozen muffins and walked over to the office. Argus made a run for his bed under my desk, and I unloaded the muffins in the break room.

Jessica and Tim came into the room, and we had our morning meeting with coffee and muffins. Argus, hearing food noises came running in and sat at attention where he could see the three of us.

"Any appointments today?" I asked Jessica.

"Nothing yet," she answered.

"I think," Tim said, "we should talk to Christina Drake's employer since she is the one who recommended that she hire us."

"That's a good idea," I said. "She can give us a little bit of background on our client."

"We'll have to do it when Christina isn't there," added Tim.

"I'll call and set it up," said Jessica as she finished off her second muffin.

Dr. Kathy Cord turned out to be a psychiatrist, and we were meeting her at five o'clock. Christina leaves work at four thirty, so we were able to talk to the doctor without our client knowing we were checking up on her.

After introductions Tim got right to the point. "How long has Christina worked for you?"

"She has been with me for ten years. She is reliable and a good receptionist."

"What is your impression of her as a person?" I asked. Sometimes the assessment of others is helpful.

"That's a tougher question," admitted Dr. Cord. "She seems guarded, but my feeling is that she's afraid if she says too much that I'll be analyzing her. As far as I know she and her husband lead a simple life."

"What about the husband?" asked Tim. "What is your impression of him?"

"I've never met the man. My impression is that he travels most of the time. Anytime we have an office gathering she comes alone."

"Any sense of friction or trouble in the relationship that you've heard?" I was growing increasingly curious about the missing man.

"I've never heard her grumble about him. Mostly she just talks about the things they do together." I noticed that she checked her watch.

"Just one more question," said Tim. He also noticed her checking her watch. "Why recommend us to Christina rather than suggest she go to the police?"

"I suggested the police, but I think she was afraid that he might be involved with something illegal and didn't want the police involved."

"Did she say what these illegal activities could be?" I asked.

"No, in fact she was rather vague about the whole thing."

"Well," said Tim passing her our business card, "we've taken up too much of your time. Thank you for seeing us. If you think of anything else, give us a call."

Chapter 24

Rhonda Shepard was wearing some outfit that was so outrageous that I couldn't place it into any time period. "Nice outfit," I said as we sat in the backroom of Erebus having coffee.

"Thanks."

"I was speaking ironically," I stated.

"You are, have always been, and will continue to be a total, complete asshole."

"It's a gift I have," I said as I sipped the coffee. We were enjoying the Kona coffee I had shipped to everyone.

"Have you been in touch with those hunky Hawaiian men of yours?"

"They are not my men," I said hoping I wasn't blushing, "but we connect through email. So what gossip have I missed?" Sometimes it's best to change the subject.

"Your friend Bitch Blair has moved out of town. One weekend she just loaded up the car and drove away."

"Excellent," I said. Judy Blair was Tim's high school girlfriend, and she hated me because I was instrumental in sending her to prison as an accessory to murder.

"And I heard that they moved Becky Simpson to the mental section of the women's prison," said Rhonda knowing I would be pleased with that bit of information.

Becky Simpson was serving a very long prison term thanks to yours truly.

"They should have sent her there decades ago. By the way I haven't seen much of your fiancé since I left for Hawaii. Is there a problem?"

"I suspect he's trying to sell the business. He's been busy with out of town meetings."

"Really? He doesn't strike me as the type to sit on the porch rocking chair," I looked at her.

"And I think he's up to something new," admitted Rhonda. "But I don't have a clue what is going on."

"Have you asked him?"

"He tells me not to worry."

"Probably good advice," I said. "I should get over to the office and do some work." Argus heard me and started for the door. I harnessed him up, said goodbye and headed to the office.

Jessica had brought the baby to work and Tim was chasing her around the office. She had grown beyond the terrible twos and was at the age where she was curious about everything. She saw me and came running to give me a hug,

"Sarah Anne is growing like a weed," I said using an overused cliché.

"And keeps us jumping," sighed Jessica.

"What are we doing today?" I asked Tim as I lowered Sarah Anne to the floor.

"I think we need to go see our client and get some more information."

"I'll make the call," I offered and went off to my office followed by Argus, who hasn't let me out of his sight since I got back.

Christina Drake's house was in what used to be called Lambert Park, one of the housing developments thrown up for shipyard workers during the war. The house was one of the small, freestanding ranch style houses with a neat and tidy lawn with daffodils beginning to blossom in the garden. It probably would look better on a sunny day, but it was raining hard and Tim and I got soaked just going from the car to the front door.

"Let me take your jackets," she said as we entered a small living room. She hung our jackets in a small closet, and I could see that it was filled with men's clothing. "Please have a seat. Can I get you some coffee?"

"That would be great," I answered for both of us. "Black for Tim and just cream for me." She went into the tiny kitchen and came back with two steaming cups of coffee. As soon as I took a sip I launched into business. "We need a list of the recent business dealings of your husband."

"He doesn't share much of his business with me. But he was at a medical convention in Boston at the convention center."

"Does he do financial planning for those in the medical field?" asked Tim.

"Not really, he does financial planning for anyone."

"I see," I said not really seeing at all. "Does he have a specific company he works for?"

"No, he really works for himself. I work to keep a steady paycheck coming in because some months he makes a lot of money and other times not so much." This was just information she had already given us. I looked around and saw a framed picture of Daniel Drake. It looked like a professional photograph that maybe he had made up for business. It was the same one she had given us earlier.

"Do you know where he was staying in Boston?"

"The Hilton. He always stays at Hiltons."

"So," I said to sum up, "your husband checked into the Boston Hilton, attended a medical convention at the Boston Convention Center where he was offering financial services, and disappeared? He hasn't attempted to contact you, he doesn't answer his phone, and he didn't share much with you about his job?"

"Yes, that's right."

"We will do our best," said Tim. When we retrieved our jackets and headed out the rain had stopped. We got into the car and Tim turned to me, "What do you think?"

"I think she doesn't seem to know much about her husband. That makes me think that something is not right."

"I think he probably took off. A handsome guy like that probably could get anyone he wants."

"And," I added, "someone who plays around a lot just might piss someone off enough to run into trouble."

"Or he could just run away."

"So what's next?" I asked, but I already knew what the next step was going to be.

"Let's take a little trip to Boston. How does a night at the Hilton sound to you?"

"It sounds good to me," I said looking forward to being in the city not sure we would learn much. An internet search turned up nothing and even Black Broker failed to find anything except his name.

Tim dropped me off at the house and I got in my car and headed to the supermarket to get something for dinner. Then I picked up a bottle of good wine and headed home. Tim and Argus were already there. Tim was filling in the blanks for Hugh. I was worried about Hugh because he was looking very pale.

"Do you feel okay?" I asked Hugh.

"I think I'm just tired. I'll be fine after a good night's sleep."

"That's probably it," I said, though I was worried and the little voice in my head was saying something I couldn't quite hear.

Chapter 25

Springtime in Boston seemed to be a week ahead of the season along the Maine coast. It was too early in the season for the swan boats in the public garden, but people were out enjoying the fine weather. Boston always feels like home to me. I spent my college years living in the Back Bay, but that's a story for another time.

Tim and I checked into the Hilton, unpacked, and headed out to the theater district to have lunch at Jacob Wirth, one of the oldest restaurants in Boston, first opening in 1868. On the way out we stopped at the front desk, showed our IDs to the clerk and told him we were looking for a missing person. He was reluctant to give out information on guests, but we might have hinted that Drake might be a victim of a crime. We did learn that there was no Daniel Drake who had reserved a room or who checked in.

"Have you ever seen this man?" I asked showing the clerk the picture of the missing Drake.

"I have a good memory for faces," said the clerk. "It's a good thing to have in this business, but I can tell you I've never seen him before. A face like that I would remember."

"Well, thank you for your time," said Tim.

My pleasure Mr. Mallory," the clerk responded, proving he did have a good memory for faces.

Lunch at Jacob Wirth's was an event. We started with a cup of their clam chowder and then had a burger and of course good German beer. We headed out to the convention center after lunch to see if anyone remembered seeing Daniel Drake, even though it was a long shot since conventions have hundreds of attendees.

"We are looking for someone who may have attended last week's medical conference," stated Tim. We were sitting in the security office of the center speaking with Julius Webb, the head of security.

"There was no medical conference here last week," he informed us. "In fact it's been over a year since we've hosted a medical conference."

"Have you by chance seen this man?" I asked knowing the answer in advance.

"No, I've never seen him," said Web, "Of course I don't pay much attention to visitors unless they become a problem."

"Well, thank you for your time," I said as we got up to leave.

"Just part of the job," Webb answered.

"Well, what do you think of that?" Tim asked me as we left the center.

"The mystery grows," I said. "There is just something about all this that is more than a bit off."

"You are right about that," Tim agreed. "Well, we've got a nice room for the night, so let's enjoy Boston."

Boston is easy to get around. The subway system is extensive, but it is slow and transferring from one line to another takes even more time. When it was time for dinner we hopped on the green line to Park Street, then the red line to South Station and then the silver line to the waterfront area. Both Tim and I love seafood so we headed to the No Name Restaurant on fishermen's wharf. It was a tossup as to which restaurant had the best clam chowder, so we figured we would need to come back to Boston and try more places that dish up clam chowder.

Having learned nothing and run up expenses for our client we decided to check out of the hotel the next morning and head home. At North Station we took the Downeaster train to Portland and picked up the car. We checked at the transportation center too and showed Drake's picture to the ticket agents but drew a blank.

When we got home Argus ran to greet us and Hugh, who had been napping on the sofa, sat up and rubbed his eyes. Hugh was pale and looked tired and hadn't been himself since he returned from Canada, and then it hit me and I saw it all.

"Hugh, that was bullshit about you being in northern Quebec. You were in Montreal in the hospital weren't you?"

"What do you mean?" but he knew I knew. "I should know better than to hide from your freaking witchcraft. I did go to northern Quebec, but back in Montreal I had a mild heart attack and they put a stent in my coronary artery."

"Mild heart attack?" I looked at him. "I don't think it was mild."

"Did you know about this?" I spun around and faced Tim.

"I thought you had enough problems, and I wanted you to relax in Hawaii."

"Just for that," I said feigning being pissed off, "you two are buying me dinner, and I'm feeling like a twin lobster dinner is in my future, and possibly a plate of steamed clams."

"You're a hard hearted bastard," said Tim but he was smiling. "Let's go."

My cousin, Monica Ashworth Twist Goulet, was sitting at my kitchen table sipping on coffee. "You've reached a dead end on your missing person haven't you?" she asked, but of course she already knew the answer.

"All we have is a picture. He doesn't have his cell phone with him, and he doesn't have a car, and no one has seen him," I told her as I passed her the photograph. "And the only thing about him I can find on the internet is a name."

She closed her eyes as she held the photo. "Something here is very wrong."

"That's what I feel, too," I agreed, "but I can't tell exactly what it is."

"He's very handsome, isn't he," she remarked. "He could be a model."

"Which makes me think he's attractive enough that women could be chasing him."

"And men being men, well you get the picture," she said as she rolled her eyes. Her ex-husband Jerry Twist, was a piece of work, and cheated on her as often as he could. "What does the wife look like?"

"She's pretty enough in an average way, but not in his league in the looks department," I said.

"That's often the case isn't it? Good looking men choose plainer looking women so they can be the pretty one in the relationship."

"That and sometimes the men like other men. Notice how well he grooms himself," I told her. "A little too much of the well-groomed look to this guy."

"So," she said as she thought about it, "he could have run off with a man or a woman. There is a little something familiar about him. Like I've seen him before."

"That's what I thought, too. I guess he must be one of those guys with the generic good looks."

Just then Tim came barreling into the kitchen. "You two have to see this," he said as he threw down a magazine in front of us.

"What am I looking at?" I asked as I looked up to Tim. "Holy crap! I see it now."

"I think we need to pay a visit to our client," said Tim.

"Yes, indeed. The sooner the better."

Chapter 26

Tim and I worked out our plan before we arrived at Christina Drake's house. I had called ahead and told her we wanted to keep her updated. We pulled up to her neat little house. She opened the door and invited us in.

"You have news for me?" she asked.

"Before we start," I said, "could I use your bathroom?"

"Of course. Let me put some coffee on."

I closed the bathroom door and slowly examined the room. I looked in the medicine cabinet, I looked under the bathroom sink, and I looked in the small linen closet. I flushed the toilet and headed back to the living room.

"What do you take in your coffee?" she asked.

"Black for Tim, and just cream for me," I answered.

"Have you found him?" she asked.

Tim took a sip of coffee. "We have a few leads. We went to Boston and checked out the Hilton, but he had never checked in."

"He hadn't made a reservation either," I said looking at her carefully.

"And," continued Tim, "no one at the convention center remembered having seen him."

"But you're still trying to find him?" she asked uneasily.

"Of course," I assured her. "We will solve the case."

"Oh, thank you," she said. "More coffee?"

"No we really need to go to another appointment," I said as we took our leave.

Dr. Kathy Cord ushered us into her office. Luckily it was after hours and Christina had gone home. "Did you find Christina's husband?" she asked.

"In a way," said Tim. "Remind me how long she's worked for you?"

"About ten years," she replied. "Why?"

"Has she ever seemed strange to you at all?" I asked.

"No, she is the perfect receptionist."

"But, you've never met the husband?" Tim put the opened magazine he had brought along and placed it in front of her. Next he placed the photograph of the missing husband next to the page.

"I don't understand," she said, but I could see the wheels turning in her head.

"There is no husband," I said. "There is no trace of anyone by that name. The photo she gave us is a photoshopped image of this male model in the magazine. She has men's clothing hanging in her closet, but I noticed that they were of different sizes, probably something she picked up in a used clothing store. The bathroom was the real giveaway," I continued. "She had only one toothbrush; there were no shaving articles, and no sign of a male presence. This is a deeply disturbed woman."

"Here I am a psychiatrist, and I didn't have a clue how sick she is."

"Why would you?" asked Tim. "She had long ago learned how to compensate and from your view she was a good receptionist."

"At least now I can give her the help she needs," said Kathy Cord. "Please send me the bill for your investigation. I was the one who urged her to contact a detective. And thank you."

"Good luck," Tim said as we got up to leave, "I hope you can help her."

"I'm going to try my best," she said.

I looked at Tim, "This is the strangest case we've ever had. Chasing an imaginary husband."

"In case you haven't noticed it," said Tim, "we attract unusual cases."

And as we headed into the office, Jessica informed us that a potential client was scheduled for tomorrow.

"Let me guess," I said. "He or she wouldn't say what they wanted."

"You've got that right. He was most insistent that he talk only to the men."

"Sounds charming," said Tim. "I think we've all had enough for the day. Let's lock up and go home.

"An excellent idea, Dad," she said as she began to pack up.

Jason Goulet is a big guy. He's well over six feet tall, and though not fat by any means, he appears to fill a room. Monica, on the other hand, is petite and the two make in interesting couple. Jason was my best friend in high school and we were in the band together. So much for the walk down Memory Lane.

"So you were searching for an imaginary husband?" asked Jason. We were sitting in my kitchen where a nice pot roast was sitting in my slow cooker. Argus, as usual, was sitting under my chair.

"We didn't know it at the time," said Tim, "but it seemed strange that we couldn't find any record of him."

"Even Black Broker came up empty," I added. I should explain the Black Broker is a computer program that searches a wide selection of data bases. It was designed for law enforcement agencies, but I was able to get a copy because the developer was a old college chum.

"I knew there was something very wrong about this investigation," admitted Monica. "But I never imagined that the object of your search didn't exist."

"We both felt it," I added, "but we didn't examine it enough."

"Maybe you are right," she sighed.

"I'm sorry I missed this case," groused Hugh Cartier. "But someone wouldn't let me do anything." He glared at Tim.

"Too soon after your heart attack. We want to keep you around for a while." Tim glared back.

"Anyway," said Jason as I got up to dish out dinner, "I'm caught up on all the alarm installations and repairs." Jason works for us putting in alarm systems and surveillance cameras. "I'd like to take a few days off and take Monica somewhere."

"Take her to Montreal," I suggested. "You can stay at the condo. I find it restful to be there."

"That's a great idea." Monica loves Montreal, as do most of us.

"So what's our next case?" asked Hugh.

"What do you mean 'our' next case," said Tim. "Who said you're ready to work?"

"I think we are going to need Hugh," I said as I set the pot roast platter down on the table. "I just have that feeling." They all looked at me. Whenever I say I feel something, everyone thinks I have a direct channel to the Universe. I wish.

Chapter 27

It was early morning and I was at the coffee pot filling my cup when I felt arms encircle me from behind. "You must be feeling better," I said to Hugh. Hugh calls me his friend with fuzzy boundaries, mostly thanks to Tim who worries that I'll be left alone if something happens to him, so he encourages Hugh to look after me. It is a bit of an unusual situation, but what the hell.

"I'm feeling much better, thank you."

"Good to see you not looking so pale," said Tim as he entered the kitchen. "Why don't we go over to Ruby's and grab some breakfast?" Ruby's is a quirky little restaurant on the waterfront that employs unusual persons.

"Sure," said Tim, "Skippy the waiter will be waiting for us and working for a big tip." We called the waiter Skippy because of his habit of skipping to and from the kitchen. We've never learned his real name.

It had rained all night and the morning was cool and wet as Tim drove us to Ruby's, and sure enough Skippy came to our table. "Oh, look it's my favorite senior citizens," he said as he poured us coffee.

"Say that again and I'll hurt you," I said as I poured cream in my cup.

"Hey, I wouldn't throw any of you guys out of bed," he said over his shoulder as he left to bring us menus.

"Bold," said Hugh. "We should take him up on his offer and see how quickly he panics."

"What if he doesn't?" asked Tim. We dropped the conversation as he returned to the table with menus.

"Don't forget that we have to swing by the house afterwards and pick up Argus," I reminded everyone.

"Argus should be on the payroll," said Tim. "He spends as much time at the office as we do."

"Okay here comes breakfast," said Hugh. "Let's mess with him." Skippy put the plates down in front of us. We looked at the plates and then passed them around, and repeated the action until we had the plates back in their original positions.

"You guys are a real treat," said Skippy shaking his head.

"You better believe it," said Hugh.

Argus was sleeping on his bed in the corner of my office as I wrote up a report on the Drake case for our files. Jessica buzzed the intercom and reminded us that we were meeting a potential client in ten minutes. "I'll be right there," I said as I got up from my desk.

Tim and Hugh were already in the conference room when I arrived. Jessica came in with me to take notes. "What's his name?" I asked.

"John Smith," read Jessica from her notes.

"John Smith? Sounds like a name you would use to check into a cheap hotel," said Tim as we waited. We heard the door to the reception room open.

"I'll go bring him in," said Jessica as she headed to the outer office. She returned with our client and the three of us did a double take because standing in the doorway was our waiter Skippy.

"Have a seat, Skip… I mean Mr. Smith," I said recovering from the surprise. "What can we do for you?"

"I've known you guys for as long as I've worked at Ruby's, and I know you are good at finding missing persons. I have some money set aside. I've been saving up so I could afford you guys."

"We have had some success," said Tim cautiously, "but not always with a happy ending."

"Anything is better than not knowing the truth," Skippy said. "And I know you all call me Skippy, so please use that name."

"Okay," I said, "since we are being informal and we've known you for years, call me Jesse, Mr. Mallory is Tim, Mr. Cartier is Hugh, and Mrs. Cooper is Jessica."

"Yes, thank you," he responded. Unlike the more bubbly personality that we see at the restaurant, he seemed subdued and nervous. About five ten, he probably weighed around one sixty, and I estimated that he was in his mid-forties, possibly younger.

"Who is this missing person?" asked Hugh.

"It's me," he said. "I'm missing."

"You're missing?" I said not sure I heard correctly. "I think we've just found you. Case solved."

"You better explain," said Tim.

"Five years ago I woke up in a hospital in Portland. Apparently I had been in a bad accident. I was found, so I was told, dazed and in a ditch. I had no identification. I was badly hurt and was in the hospital for five weeks while I had surgeries and learned to walk and talk again. I recovered, but I never got my memory back. I want to know who I am."

"Permanent amnesia is rare, so I've been told," said Hugh. "Usually some memories come back."

"Not in my case," Skippy replied looking upset. "I just want to know who I am." He broke down crying.

"We'll take your case," I promised putting my hand on his shoulder. "We'll find out who you are."

"Thank you," he said drying his tears. "How much will it cost?"

"We'll need a substantial retainer," I said nodding to Jessica. "A dollar should about cover it. The balance will be due at the end of the investigation. That will be another dollar."

I wasn't prepared for his reaction because he got up and threw his arms around me sobbing. "Thank you; you don't know what it means to me."

"Actually we do," said Hugh. "Tim went missing a few years ago and we finally found him."

"Being lost is a terrible thing," added Tim.

"You say you have no memories," I asked. "Do you ever have vivid dreams?"

"Actually I do, why?"

"They may be clues as to who you are. Take a notepad and keep it next to your bed," I suggested. "Write down any details you remember."

"I will," he replied. I was afraid he would start crying again.

"Jessica will go over the forms with you, if you'd like to follow her to the outer office."

"What do you think of that?" asked Tim as soon as Skippy was out of the room.

"Very emotional," I said. "But there must be a clue out there somewhere."

"What do the spirits tell you?" asked Hugh.

"They tell me you're a wise ass," I responded. "My intuition, on the other hand, says we'll find him an identity."

"Good enough for me," said Tim.

"Me, too," agreed Hugh.

Chapter 28

Viola Vickner, our local Pagan priestess, was working the counter at Erebus when I entered with Argus. "Bright blessings, Jesse" she said as her usual greeting. Argus, hearing her voice went running to her, knowing she keeps doggie biscuits under the counter.

"Where's the other witch?" I asked.

"I heard that!" yelled Rhonda from the back room. "You better have some muffins with you."

"Sorry," I said, "I've only got a coffee cake with me."

"Cake? You have cake? You are a saint."

"Saint Jesse, just doesn't sound right," I shot back. I put the cake on the counter and Rhonda came out with a knife and paper plates. Today she was wearing the female version of a 1970s leisure suit.

"If I'd known it was disco fever day, I would have dressed for it. Where's the mirror ball?

"Very funny. You want something, don't you?" she asked suspiciously.

"What makes you think that?" I asked innocently.

"You bringing coffee cake for one." She cut three pieces and passed one to Viola and one to me. "What do you want?"

"Well…" I started to say.

"I knew it," she said before I could finish. Viola was looking back and forth from me to Rhonda like she was watching a tennis game. "You usually bring a few muffins, but today you brought a whole coffee cake. What's up?"

"You're good friends with Ruby Baker, right?" I asked. Ruby owns Ruby's Restaurant. Ruby is the queen of soul food, something we in Bath had never had until she moved here years ago and set up her restaurant on the water front.

"Yes, and boy can that woman cook. What about her?"

"I need you to find out all you can about John Smith, the waiter we call Skippy."

"That's his name? Really?"

"It's a long story," I said, "and I'm not at liberty to say more."

"Why don't you ask her yourself?" asked Rhonda.

"I don't want him to know I'm checking up on him," I explained. "I'll explain it all at some point."

"This is a case you're working on, isn't it?"

"Maybe," I answered. Viola just looked at us, shook her head, and headed into the back room. Argus followed her.

"Fine, the store opens in an hour. I'll run down to the waterfront and talk to her. Viola can watch the store if I'm not back. I'll stop back at your office after I talk to her. What do you need to know?"

"I'd like to know what he told her when he applied for the job. Also why she hired him, and if he needed training or if being a waiter came naturally to him. And anything else she's noticed about him," I explained.

"This is getting interesting," she said hoping I'd explain more.

"And her observation about the type of person he is."

"So basically," she said looking at me, "you want to know everything about him."

"Basically, yes."

"Can I tell her that it's you who wants the information?" asked Rhonda.

"Yes, and that I don't want Skippy to know I'm asking about him."

I called Argus who came running, and we headed up the street to the office.

As I entered the office Sarah Anne came running up to give me a hug, "Gramps," she said. She calls me gramps and Tim she calls grandpa.

"Sorry," said Jessica. "I had to bring her in. Derek's mother is coming over to pick her up. Daycare is closed for the day."

"You don't need to apologize," I said. "I'm always happy to see her. Where's Tim?"

"He went out to meet Jason. Someone wants a security camera installed by their house."

"I'll be in my office running Black Broker through its paces. Where's Hugh?"

"He ran over to the police station to see Derek," she explained.

Skippy was rather vague about when he had been admitted to the hospital, so I ran a search for missing persons in Maine for the last five years to see if any of them matched up with Skippy, but I knew nothing would turn up. The hospital would have contacted the police when he showed up.

A half hour later I had a list of five persons, none of whom matched up with Skippy's description. I knew running a nationwide search would result in a list of thousands and thousands of names and would be almost useless.

"Where's the old dude?" I heard Rhonda ask Jessica in the outer office. Jessica pointed to my office and Rhonda came sailing in. "Well, that was interesting."

"How so?" I asked. Rhonda took a seat.

"Here's the scoop," she said looking pleased. "He showed up one day and applied for a job. Ruby said he started as a dish washer but when one of the waitresses left he asked if he could try it. She said he was a natural. Didn't even need training."

"Sounds like he has done this before," I said stating the obvious.

"There's more. She let him sleep in the backroom until he saved up enough to rent a room. He told her he was in a bad accident and was slowly recovering. According to her he's quiet and polite and enjoys being a waiter. She said he also likes to flirt with the male customers."

"No kidding," I said.

"Other than that, there isn't much more she could tell me," said Rhonda.

"Well, thanks for trying. The clue here is that he's been a waiter before."

"So," she asked, "you are looking for a missing waiter?"

"Not necessarily," I replied. "He may have worked his way through college as a waiter and for all we know he could be a rocket scientist." That gave me an idea. What was his level of education? I'd have to test that out.

"And your super-duper computer program isn't helping?" Rhonda asked.

"I need to feed it information, and right now I don't have enough information to do a thorough search."

"Well, I need to get back to the store before Viola starts selling caldrons and broomsticks."

Chapter 29

Just to be sure that I tried everything I fed Black Broker the information I had so far. I added the waiter information and did a nationwide search and as I suspected it came up with too many names to even sift through.

"How's it going?" asked Tim sticking his head into my office.

"Black Broker is a bust," I answered getting up from my desk. "I need more information to set parameters in the search. So far I have a list of six hundred names and Black Broker is still spitting out more names."

"You sound a little tense," said Tim closing the office door and locking it. "I think you need some relaxation, and no one is here at the moment."

"Relaxation would be most welcome," I said clearing off my desk.

Black Broker finished searching for missing men, and I was no closer to finding anything more than I was before. I picked up the phone and called Skippy. He agreed to come to the office once the lunch crowd had left.

I spent the rest of the morning typing out reports, and then Monica called. "Well, this is a surprise," I said. "You don't often call me at work."

"I thought you might need help."

"I can use all the help I can get," I said truthfully. "I'm trying to figure out a case, and I'm not having much luck."

"You're looking for someone, aren't you?" she asked.

"I would ask you how you knew, but I already know the answer."

"This time it's just a guess. But I think there must be a twist to this case."

"Why don't you stop by tomorrow, and I'll fill you in," I said. I'm not above seeking help from the Universe.

Jessica and Tim returned bringing good Maine Italian sandwiches for our lunch. Back in New Hampshire it was impossible to find these sandwiches, and I missed them. There had been attempts to bring Maine style sandwich shops to the state, but each one failed.

"Any progress?" asked Jessica as we sat in the break room.

"Not so far," I answered. "Skippy is coming over this afternoon and I'll have more information, I hope."

"This must be our hardest case," said Tim.

"It certainly is different," added Jessica.

"Well," I replied, "someone somewhere is missing a son or a brother, or a boyfriend or even a husband."

"You think Skippy has a wife?" asked Tim sounding incredulous.

"You had one," I fired back.

"I was confused," he laughed.

"My point being," I continued, "that someone is missing him."

"You'll find out who he is," Jessica stated. I wasn't as confident.

Skippy, aka John Smith, sat in the conference room. Tim and Jessica sat on one side of the table and I sat on the other side with Skippy. "I'll need the time frame when you were in the hospital," I said and he gave it as Jessica took notes. "Was it Maine Medical?"

"Yes, I have no idea how I got there," he said shaking his head.

"The hospital won't give out any information," stated Tim. "But I'll call my friends at the Portland Police and check out the report."

"Good idea," I said. "Now Skippy. I understand that you didn't need any instructions on how to be a waiter."

"It seemed very natural to me," he said. "And I enjoy the work."

"Tell me about yourself," I asked. "What do you read? What do you do for entertainment? What about your social life?"

"Jeez, Jesse, you don't want much," he replied. "I read Rex Stout, Agatha Christie. I like the Victorian poets, at least some of them, others are dreary. I watch TV, mostly PBS. My friends all work at Ruby's."

"Victorian poets and PBS," repeated Tim. "Do you think you went to college?"

"Well, I seem to know a lot of things, but I have no idea."

"I have the feeling," I said following my intuition, "that the average person isn't a fan of Victorian poetry. By the way, do you prefer American poets or English poets?"

Skippy paused for a moment thinking it over. "I like the English Victorian poets, but I also like the American poets of the early Modern Period."

Well that settled the question for me. He had clearly gone to college and attended at least some literature classes. "Are you writing down your dreams?" I asked.

"I am now. I'm also writing down some of the recurring dream images. But it's only been a few days."

Tim took over the interview. "We're going to Portland to talk to the police who found you, and let's meet again at the end of the week and bring your list of dreams."

"You really think dreams will help?"

"I believe some of the images will give us some context," I said.

"I can't thank you enough," said Skippy as he got up to leave. "You guys are great."

"Don't you forget it," I shot back.

Hugh had gone home because he wasn't feeling well, I was getting concerned about his health. True, he was looking better, but he tired easily. I could relate to that because chemo had wiped me out.

He was sleeping on the sofa when Tim and I returned home. Argus had snuggled up with him on the sofa. Hugh opened his eyes.

"How are you feeling?" Tim questioned Hugh.

"I feel fine, but I tire easily," he responded.

"I know the feeling," I said. "Anything we can do?"

"How about some comfort food."

"That sounds good," Hugh replied.

"I have a one pot recipe I want to try out," I said to both of them. I'll go to the store and pick up what I need."

"Take your time," said Tim. "I'll look after this one."

Chapter 30

Portland was rainy and I loved wandering around its crooked streets, but we were here for business, so we headed off to the police station. Tim, as a former police chief seems to know everyone in law enforcement so it didn't take us long before we were sitting in the office of detective Darius Bristle.

"Good to see that retirement agrees with you, Tim," said Darius as he indicated two chairs in front of his desk.

"Darius, this is Jesse my partner," Tim introduced us. I didn't detect a negative reaction so I sat back and relaxed.

"Here are the files if you want to look them over," he said as he passed the files to Tim. "I was the one on the case."

"Why don't you tell us what you remember," I suggested.

"A jogger up on the Eastern Promenade came across what he thought was a body and called 911. I arrived before the ambulance and determined that he was still alive. He was covered with blood. He was in a ditch by the road and we figured he had been hit by a car.

"It was several days before we could question him, but he had no memory of the accident. The doctors said he should begin to regain his memory, but it didn't happen."

"Could he have been hit on purpose?" I asked. As I said it I felt like I was on the right path.

"Given the speed limit and the clear visibility we think it probably was on purpose or most likely a drunk driver, rather than accidental," said Darius thinking back on the event.

"Any other clues?" asked Tim.

"We sent out a request to the body shops to report any damaged cars from around that time period, but nothing came up. He had no wallet or identification. The only jewelry he had on was a fairly elaborate cross."

"Cross or crucifix?" I asked.

"What's the difference?" asked Darius.

"A cross is plain, mostly used by protestants, the crucifix has an image of Jesus' body on the cross, typical of Anglo Catholics and Roman Catholics," I said.

"This was really neither," Darius continued. "It had the Jesus image but it was engraved. Do you think that is significant?"

"Not really," I admitted. "Did he have a watch?"

"He had one of the more moderately priced watches. I'd say it was under three hundred dollars."

"So it wasn't a cheap department store watch?" asked Tim.

"It was a Seiko chronometer," I added as I read the report. "a really nice watch.." I read more of the report. "Fashion brand name clothing, too. I'm guessing he wasn't just a waiter."

"Any inscription on the watch?" asked Tim.

"HBS 13:16," I read from the report.

"It's a Bible quote," said Darius. "I looked it up and it's a quote about serving others."

"So," mused Tim, "we have a cross and a watch with a Bible inscription. He must have been active in some religious movement."

"Skippy doesn't seem the religious type," I said.

"No, but neither do you, yet you go to church every Sunday and sing in the choir."

"Quiet," I shot back. "You'll spoil my image."

Darius laughed at that. "I'm not sure any of this will help," he continued seriously.

"Maybe," I replied. "Maybe not. There doesn't seem to be much else in this report to help."

"Well, thanks for your help," Tim said to Darius. "We should do lunch soon."

"I'd like that," said Darius. "Take care and good luck."

We left the police station and unfurled our umbrellas and headed down to the waterfront in the rain. The rain and the sea air combined and the air smelled both fresh and salty. I love the combination of dark and cold outside and the warmth and light inside. There are so many good restaurants in the Old Port area, but we both were in the mood for seafood, so we headed off to Gilbert's Chowder House for clam chowder and a fried scallop lunch.

"You must have some feeling about the case," Tim asked me as we were served beer while we waited for chowder.

"My gut tells me that the outfit he was found in is significant. He was well dressed and wearing a bronze cross and a quality watch, yet he had no wallet or identification. He clearly doesn't appear to be homeless. He belongs somewhere, and someone is missing him. And it begs the question 'what happened to his wallet?' So where does that all leave us?"

"Total amnesia is so rare," said Tim as we were served our chowder, "that he could be faking."

"Why fake amnesia? It might be a ploy if you were running from something and wanted to start a new life, but if that was the case why hire us to find his identity. I don't think he has total amnesia."

"You don't?" asked Tim looking at me.

"I think he remembers more than he realizes. He knew he had the skills to be a waiter, and he said he experiences dream fragments that make no sense, but I think they may be clues if we can put them together."

"That was a good suggestion you made having him write down his dreams," complimented Tim.

"See, I'm not just another pretty face." Fortunately our lunch arrived before Tim could respond.

When we got back to the office Hugh was filling in for Jessica at the front desk. "Where's Jessica?" asked Tim with concern in his voice.

"She went to pick up Sarah Anne from day care. It seems there was some type of illness going around so they closed day care for a few days to keep the sickness from spreading."

"A good idea," I said. "Remember the Hong Kong flu that was going around when we were in high school. It wiped out the faculty and they had to bring in college students to substitute."

"How do you remember things so far back?" asked Tim.

"It's a gift," I replied not knowing how that piece of the past popped into my head.

"What did you learn?" asked Hugh. "Anything helpful?"

"We found out a few things," answered Tim. "Not sure how helpful any of it will be."

"I'm going to type up my notes before I forget what I wrote down. When I finish why don't we sit down in the conference room and go over the findings," I suggested. "See if we can put together the pieces."

"I'll run down to the coffee shop," offered Hugh, "and bring back some lattes and pastries."

"Excellent," I said. "I could use a nice hot latte."

Chapter 31

The three of us sat in the conference room sipping our lattes as I passed out my typed notes. "Take a few minutes and look them over," I said, "and see what you think."

"I'm not sure any of this adds up to anything," remarked Hugh as he finished reading the notes.

"I think they may make sense when we find out who Skippy is," I said, "but as for helping us find his identity I'm not sure any of this helps."

"Well," suggested Tim, "let's review all we know so far."

"According to what Skippy has told us and what we've learned from the police report," I began, "Skippy was hit by a car somewhere on the Eastern Prom in Portland. It was a hit and run. He was beside the road and someone walking her dog saw him and called for help. He was taken to Maine Medical Center. He remembers nothing about the accident and nothing before that. He had no identification."

"Yet," spoke Hugh, "amnesia usually isn't permanent."

"From what little I know about it," added Tim. "Once a person is exposed to their past, they begin to remember things."

"Which is why," I continued, "we need to find out who Skippy really is. Once he has some information about his past, exposure to those events may trigger memory."

"We've got very little to go on," said Hugh.

"His clothing suggests he was well off," I said. "His knowledge of literature tells me he probably went to college, or at the very least loves reading. At first I thought he was probably a waiter because he needed very little training at Ruby's, plus the fact that he sought out a job as a waiter. But his clothing and the watch he wore suggests he was well off."

"Maybe he was just a successful waiter," suggested Hugh.

"That is possible of course," I conceded.

"So what next?" asked Tim.

"I'd like to see the medical report but we know the hospital won't give it to us," I said.

"I'm not sure reading medical jargon will help us."

"No, but Jack Dodd at church is a medical doctor and could probably help us," I said. "But I know they won't release it."

"Looking at the time," said Tim, "I think we should wrap up work for today."

"Not a bad idea," I agreed. "You guys go ahead. I need to stop at the store and get something for dinner."

Argus, who had been sleeping in my lap, jumped up when he heard the word 'dinner.' The word 'no' he doesn't understand, but any word related to food he understands.

The rain had stopped and the sun had returned. I was happy to be back in Bath, but I missed Hawaii and the friends I had made there. I was keeping in touch with Johnny and Travis through social media and email, but it wasn't the same. I decided to make a Hawaiian dish of spam and cabbage for dinner. For one thing I wanted to see Tim and Hugh's reaction to spam. It might be popular in Hawaii, but Maine was a different story. And I really like the dish.

"How do you find a missing person when no one has reported a missing man?" asked Hugh. He and Tim were sitting at the kitchen table while I was cooking. Argus, of course, was watching me cook. We were still hashing ideas around.

"Probably because when he disappeared," I said as the little voice in my head was yelling at me, "it was thought that he wanted to disappear. Adults run away all the time." The little voice in my head was still yelling at me, but I couldn't quite understand what it was saying. Sometimes I hate that little voice.

"Can't you use your magic powers to figure this out?" asked Hugh.

"If I had magic powers, what makes you think I'd be hanging out with your sorry asses?"

"Harsh," said Tim as I finished cooking up the spam and cabbage dinner.

"Okay let me rephrase that," amended Hugh. "What does your intuition say?"

"Nothing yet. I need more information before my brain can process any ideas. Now who's ready for spam and cabbage?" I said as I dished the meal onto the plates.

"You're kidding, right?" commented Tim.

"Actually this is good," said Hugh as he took a tentative taste.

"Surprisingly not bad," admitted Tim.

"Now," I suggested, "let's talk about something else so we can enjoy dinner."

I sat up in bed "So what's the plan of the day?" I asked Tim. Both Hugh and Tim were in varied states of undress, which made it hard to focus on the coming day.

"Breakfast at Ruby's with our favorite waiter," said Tim shedding his clothes and heading into the shower. "Anyone want to join me and save water?"

"I'm in," said Hugh.

"Me, too," I added.

Later, fresh, clean, and relaxed, the three of us headed to Ruby's. The waterfront was foggy which added a spooky atmosphere to the morning. Once we ordered breakfast Skippy joined us by prearrangement. "Maria is covering my tables," he informed us when he sat down with us, "so I can talk."

"What I'd like to know," I said, "is if you've had any dreams that you've written down?"

"I've had a few, but I don't think they'll be helpful," he answered. "Just fragments of what I can remember after I wake up."

"You never know," I said. "Sometimes you might think that some small detail couldn't possibly be important, so tell us what you wrote down."

"Well then," Skippy began, "In one of the dreams I was surrounded by men and had a real sense of well-being."

"Sounds like a nice dream," sighed Hugh. I shot him a look.

"And in another," continued Skippy, "I was standing in front of a large stone building."

"Was it a public type of building," asked Tim. "Something like a city hall, court house, or maybe a school or library?"

"I'm not sure."

"What was your feeling about the building," I asked.

"Maybe more like a school or library," Skippy added.

"Anything else?" asked Hugh.

"Just a feeling of being in a big field out in the country. That's it," said Skippy. "Now I need to get back to work. I'll bring over more coffee."

Both Hugh and Tim looked at me as soon as Skippy left the table. "What?" I asked.

"You know," said Tim looking up at the ceiling. "Woo woo."

"If you mean did I have any psychic breakthrough about his dreams? The answer is no." That wasn't entirely true, I did have a deep feeling there were clues, but I had no evidence, nor had I had time to process these feelings. Still there was something stirring in the back of my mind that seemed to be taking shape. If only I could see the situation clearly in my mind. But, of course, I couldn't.

Chapter 32

Rhonda was having a party to celebrate my return, even though I had been back for more than a month now. Rhonda and Jackson have a huge house along the river front. The river was higher than I've ever seen it. The spring ice melt, plus all the rain had contributed to the river swell. Fortunately the house was set up on a hill far from the rising waters. I had seen old photographs of flooding downtown, but that was back in the 1930s.

It was supposed to be a surprise. Rhonda had only said it was a get-together, but because of my sixth sense, or whatever you want to call it, I don't get a lot of surprises. As I walked into the house, followed by Hugh and Tim, I saw the huge banner in their rather large living room that said "Welcome Back Jesse."

I looked around and the room was filled with the usual suspects, plus two guys I hadn't seen in almost a year. Parker Reed was as handsome as ever, and beside him was Billy Simpson. Since Billy had given up drink, he was glowing with health. I went over and both of them hugged me.

"Is that a gun in your pocket?" I asked Parker once he released me.

"Sure," he shot back. "Want to see it?"

"I've seen it," I replied and we all laughed.

"Our ship had to go in for repairs," said Billy. "So we have a few weeks off."

"Great," I said. "I've missed you both."

Jackson Bennett, Rhonda's fiancé, spotted me and came over. He always looks the same. White hair with every strand in place, jacket and tie in the latest style, and well-groomed.

"Welcome back, Jesse," he said. "Sorry I couldn't make it to Honolulu with Rhonda."

"We had a good time," I said.

"I was in business talks about buying out another insurance company," he explained.

"Shouldn't you be getting ready for retirement?" I asked.

"I'm never going to retire," he said. "You know you retire and you are dead within a year."

"I've been retired for almost ten years," I said. "And I retired at fifty-five."

"You didn't retire," he said. "You've worked at something since you left teaching, and now you are a detective."

"I guess you're right," I admitted. Being self employed didn't seem like real work, especially since Tim and I only have to take cases that interest us.

"Could I have your attention, please," yelled my neighbor Beth White, who looks no more like a rabbi than I look like Justin Timberlake. "I've been asked to give a brief prayer before dinner."

Once the prayer for thanksgiving was over the caterers brought in the food for the buffet. I was relieved because Rhonda can't cook for crap, though I suspect that her refusal to learn to cook is because she rebels against traditional female roles. Good for her.

"We've missed you at church," said the Reverend Mary Bailey. "I'm glad you are back. The choir could use you."

"It's about to wrap up for the season," I said, "though I'll be there for the last choir Sunday."

I filled my plate with food at the buffet. I judge food by my own standards. Is it better than I can make, or is my food better? The food here seemed to fall into each of those categories. Some of the dishes were better than I could make and some not. One thing I knew for sure was that there would be cake for dessert. Rhonda loves cake. Have I said that before?

I was right, there was cake for dessert. She had ordered a huge chocolate cake. I did a double take when I saw that the cake said 'Happy Birthday Jesse.' My birthday was months ago.

"Hey, everyone," yelled Rhonda. "I want to wish Jesse a happy birthday today because he was away on his real birthday."

I had to suffer through a rendition of "Happy Birthday" sung by mostly non-singers.

"Jackson, bring out Jesse's present," yelled Rhonda.

Jackson left and returned with a strange looking box. Everyone gathered around as if they knew what the present was. Jackson set the box on the table, and I took off the cover. I couldn't believe my eyes.

"Do you like it?" asked Rhonda.

"I love it," I answered. "And so will Argus." In the box was a squirming pug puppy who licked my hand as I took him out of the box. He was wearing a tiny tee shirt that sported the name Sparky. I held him close as he licked my face.

"I think he likes you," said Tim.

"Did you know about this?" I asked Tim.

"I sure did. It was hard to keep it a secret I have to say."

The day turned out to be a very good day.

I was moved to see how many friends showed up for my party, and I thanked each one of them before I left. As I left I knew someone was missing, but I couldn't think who and then it came to me. My old high school English teacher, Beatrice Lafond. I started to panic. Had she passed away while I was sunning myself on Waikiki beach? "Where's Mrs. Lafond?" I asked Tim.

"She's fine," said Tim. "She doesn't go out at night. They discourage night trips at the home. She sends her best and wants to see you as soon as you are ready."

Tim drove me home with a sleeping Sparky in my arms.

The next morning when I woke up, Tim was already up and making coffee. Argus and Sparky were curled up together sleeping on the bed. So much for worrying how Argus would like another dog in his home. Argus saw me stirring and jumped out to go outside for his business and more importantly he was ready for feeding time. Sparky took his cue from Argus and rushed outside where they both did their business. I put down two bowls of food and their bowls were empty in record time.

Tim poured me a cup of coffee and shortly Hugh came in to make breakfast. "I'm not sure the health department would approve of you cooking with your bathrobe open," I told Hugh.

"Should I go get dressed?" he asked.

"Absolutely not," I replied. "Just letting you know that I noticed." Both Tim and Hugh are a bit of exhibitionists. But then again if you have it, flaunt it. I, on the other hand, am not so bold.

"What's up today?" I asked.

"Well. It is Sunday, so church at ten, then brunch, and I thought we'd go see old lady Lafond," Tim suggested.

"Sounds okay to me," I said. "This is the last Sunday for choir, so I'm free until September."

"I hope you people are singing something good," remarked Hugh.

"We always sing something good," I replied.

Chapter 33

The Sagadahoc Nursing Home had been home to Beatrice Lafond for the past ten years, set in a wooded area of town it seemed pleasant enough. Mrs. Lafond was sitting in the solarium when Tim and I arrived.

"Jesse, it's about time you came to see me," she said looking up from her book. "You always were late to class."

"I was never late for your class," I protested.

"Maybe I disremember," she conceded with a laugh. "Please sit down. I don't like looking up at visitors." We took the two empty seats in front of her.

"Bah, your memory is better than mine," I responded.

"Maybe it was Timothy who was always late. Hanging out with that Blair girl."

"Don't remind me," said Tim.

"I could have predicted how she would turn out," said Mrs. Lafond. "You, on the other hand," she said to me, "were a total surprise. I never would have guessed you would become an English teacher. Tim, I knew would be successful in anything he did."

"How are you?" I asked to change the subject.

"I'm old, that's how I am. I'm glad you're back. I hope Hawaii was a good place for you to recover. I can't imagine how awful chemo was for you."

"The treatments weren't bad," I told her, "it was the aftermath. A few days after treatment I could barely get out of bed. And just as I began to feel better it was time for another treatment. But I can't complain because I'm healthy now."

"I hear you have a new addition to your family," she said referring to Sparky.

"He's a winner," I said. "It was a total surprise."

We talked on for a bit until we could tell she was tiring out. We said our goodbyes and promised to visit again soon. The fact was I was tired out, too, so when we arrived home I headed to the bed for a nap. Argus and Sparky, not wanting to be left out, jumped up on the bed, circled three times, and cuddled up to me.

I do some of my best detective work in that twilight time between awake and asleep. I closed my eyes and tried to picture the images that Skippy had described: groups of men, stone building, and open fields. I knew these were significant, but I had no breakthrough.

My meditations were interrupted by the phone. I looked at the caller ID and sighed. "Hello, Mother," I said into the phone expecting a conversation of nonsense.

"Jesse, I hope I haven't caught you at a bad time? I just wanted to touch base and see how you are doing. I'm glad you're back home. Your father and I may come up in August."

"Who is this?" I asked. This couldn't be my mother because whoever was on the other end of the phone didn't sound crazy.

"Very funny. I'll put your father on the line."

"Hi, son," said my father. I could tell there was something in his voice.

"What's going on?" I asked. "Mother sounds normal."

"The operation open up the blood flow to her brain, plus some medication helps."

"I'm not crazy," yelled my mother in the background.

"There we go," I said into the phone. "That's more like it."

"Nothing is perfect," he said to me, "but it's better."

"You tell my grandson he needs to come for a visit," she yelled. "And your father's crazy."

"I see what you mean. Are you coming for a visit this summer?" I asked.

"Yes, we'll be staying at the new hotel in town. I'll let you go."

"Love you both," I said and ended the call.

Monica and I were sitting in the coffee shop while Brian Stillwater was whipping up two lattes, which he brought over to the table. "So these are the fragments of his dreams," I said as I passed her a list of Skippy's dreams.

"I'm sure they are significant," she agreed as she looked at the list. "But my gut feeling is that you're missing the real clue."

"That's my feeling, too," I admitted. "But I've no idea what I'm missing"

"I think when you find the clue, the images will fall into place."

"I can't imagine," I said, "what it's like not to know who you are. It was hard enough for me when I felt disoriented."

"And you ran away to Hawaii."

"I went to recover," I protested. "I didn't run away."

"You forget who you are talking to, 'Cuz."

"Anyway," I said to get back to the main subject, "what else do you see on the list?"

She thought about it for a moment. "These images that seem unrelated actually go together."

"Okay, stone buildings, open field, and men. What does it mean?"

"You forgot the sense of well-being he had in his dreams."

"I guess I did. It still doesn't help. I really could use Grandma's help," I sighed.

"Who knows," mused Monica, "maybe she is helping on the other side."

"Well, maybe, but…"

"But," said Monica finishing my sentence, "we are skeptics. Give me a break. I know you like to think you are a skeptic, so people won't think you're crazy. But that ship has sailed."

"Sail this," I said adding a finger gesture.

"Nice attitude," she laughed. "Now it would be a good idea if just you and I sat down with Skippy."

"Let's go,"

It was between breakfast and lunch at Ruby's and Skippy was able to sit down with us. "Monica, whom you've waited on before is my close cousin," I told Skippy as he sat down three cups of coffee. Monica and I sipped the coffee slowly since we had just finished our lattes at the coffee shop.

"How is the search going?" Skippy asked with a hopeful look.

"We're not making much progress," I said.

"But we are getting closer," said Monica, more to keep up his spirits than stating the truth.

"I thought we would try something," Monica suggested. "Close your eyes, and empty your mind, and as we ask questions tell us what pops into your head."

Skippy did as he was told. "How do you see yourself dressed?" I asked.

"I'm wearing some type of brown hoodie," he said looking somewhat surprised at what he imagined.

"Look around you," added Monica, "what do you see?"

"I see rolling hills with something growing. It looks like vines. Maybe a vineyard? I can't tell. I see some buildings far off in the distance by a pond." His eyes flew open with a confused look. "Do you think I'm seeing something from my life?"

"Yes, I do," I answered. "But whether the images are actual or symbolic, it's hard to tell."

"What did you feel when you saw the images?" asked Monica.

"A sense of peace," he answered. "I felt I belonged."

"Try to keep those images in your mind," I suggested, "and see if anything else comes to you. Now we should let you get back to work."

As we were about to leave Ruby came running into the dining room in a panic. "My cook just quit," she said in a panic. "Lunch will begin in an hour. What am I going to do?"

"I'll do it," said Skippy. "I can fill in."

We all looked at him as if he had lost his mind. "You can cook?" I asked.

"I think I can. I think I've cooked for a big crowd before."

"Then you better see what you can do," said Ruby. "I don't have much choice."

Somewhere in the recesses of my mind puzzle pieces were falling into place, but I couldn't see the whole picture yet.

Chapter 34

It was warm and sunny and we had closed the office for lunch. Tim, Jessica, Hugh, and I went over to Ruby's for lunch to see how Skippy was as a cook."

Ruby herself took us to a table. "He's been wasting his talent being a waiter. He is an excellent cook. He made me run out for some groceries because he wanted to make a special for lunch and I recommend it."

"What's the special?" asked Jessica.

"Beef burgundy," she said. "Shall I put in your orders?" We all ordered the special just to see how good of a cook Skippy was.

"Oh, my!" said Jessica. "This is so good."

"It's even better than yours," Tim said to me.

"Where are you sleeping tonight?" I asked. But I had to agree this was the best I've ever had. Skippy better cough up the recipe or I'd have to beat it out of him.

"What do you think?" asked Ruby as she came over to clear our table once we had finished lunch.

We all had varying degrees of praise for the meal. Ruby brought over complimentary Irish coffee for our table.

"Okay," I said as I sipped my coffee. "We need to review what we have so far for clues."

"Obviously he's cooked before, probably as a chef or head cook," said Tim.

"Let me read you a list of the images he's come up with in both dreams and thoughts," I said. "Stone building, open fields, a possible vineyard, brown hoodie, feelings of belonging."

"It sounds like he might have been a cook for a restaurant run as part of a vineyard," suggested Jessica.

"I agree," chimed in Hugh.

"Let me put that info into Black Broker and see what we come up with. Hopefully we have enough information to begin a real search," I said. But at the time I had missed the best clue that would solve the mystery of 'who the hell was Skippy?'

Back at the office I fed Black Broker the information that we had garnered so far, and I was rewarded with a message that said "No Information Found." Apparently there were so many vineyards that the program was unable to process. I reentered the information and limited the search to vineyards in Maine and New Hampshire, and included those with restaurants. I learned that there were no vineyards with restaurants in either state. I did find one in Connecticut, but that failed to be helpful. I did call them and ask if they had a missing cook, but their cook had been employed there for years and was present and accounted for. I was getting frustrated and when I looked at the clock it was time to leave and plan something for dinner.

I tried to think of something for dinner since Jay and his partner Steven would be joining us for dinner. My son loves what I cook, but I wasn't feeling too inspired, so I just bought some ground beef, a can of crushed tomatoes, and egg noodles, and some frozen corn to make a one pot dinner. I had my doubts, but as it was cooking it smelled good. White trash cooking.

When Jay and Steven arrived I was in the kitchen and Hugh and Tim were serving up drinks in the living room. Jay came in with a glass of wine for me and gave me a hug. "I don't see enough of you, Dad. It seems like we are always busy."

"I remember what it's like to be an English teacher. Correcting, lesson planning, correcting. Did I mention all the correcting?"

"I had a call from Grandma," he said after we agreed on too much time on correcting. "She seemed sane."

"I had a call, too. I think clearing out her arteries helped quite a bit."

"Do you think some of it was acting?" he asked. "Seems like she took pride in being eccentric."

"Yes, I do. When I was a kid she always said that when she got old she was going to be an interesting old lady. Some of it, however," I said, "is because she is bat-shit crazy."

"When is dinner?"asked Hugh as he came into the kitchen. "I'm starved."

"It's about ready, so start herding everyone in."

"So what case are you working on now?" Steven asked once we had all sat down.

"We are looking for a missing person," Tim explained. "Or rather we are trying to establish the true identity of our client."

We didn't tell anyone who the client was to protect Skippy's privacy. "But we are not doing too well," I said. "There isn't much to go on and no one seems to have reported him missing."

"You're talking about Skippy, aren't you?"said Jay.

"How did you know?" asked Hugh.

"Skippy hangs out with us. He told us all about his amnesia."

"What did he tell you?" I asked Jay and Steven. "Anything that might be a clue?"

"He seems well educated, so we speculated that he went to college," added Steven.

"He said something about a college with red brick buildings, but he didn't know if that was a memory or just something he saw once," Jay informed us.

"Well, that's one more clue that we didn't have before," said Hugh.

"Except that could describe any college anywhere," I said.

"Too true," said Tim. "We really are at a standstill."

"I refuse to give up," I said, though I was afraid Tim was right. Even my intuition, which usually at least points me to a clue, didn't seem to be engaged in this search.

"What's for dessert?" asked Jay seeing that I was beating myself up about the case.

"Chocolate mousse," I said. "I just have to whip up some cream for the topping."

"Dinner, by the way," said Steven, "was very good. Jay's been trying to cook like you, and he's doing a good job."

"I have a good teacher," said Jay looking at me.

"And a nice glass of port after dessert would be a good idea," added Tim.

Later as I was lying in bed looking up at the ceiling the little voice in my head kept saying over and over "what was he wearing?" Tim was sleeping away. I always envy people who are good sleepers.

"What was he wearing?" I asked myself and then it hit me. It was all there and it was so clear. "Tim, wake up," I said shaking him.

"What's wrong?" he asked rubbing his eyes.

"I'm so stupid," I said. "All the clues were there and the answer was so clear that I didn't give it a second thought."

"What are you talking about?" Tim was still half awake.

"It's the cross he was wearing when they found him. That's the clue. Remember how ornate it was?"

"I guess so," he answered.

"All the other images fit with the cross," I said not sure that I could get back to sleep after this.

"I don't get it," said Tim. "Get some sleep and we'll deal with it in the morning."

Chapter 35

The morning was still dark, but red streaks were beginning to show in the sky. Tim was awake and in the shower. I went into Hugh's room and looked at him. Since his heart trouble I always dread going in to check on him. What if he isn't breathing? But I could see his chest rising and falling so I knew he was alive. I went over to wake him.

"Good morning," I said. "Time to get up."

He threw back the covers and grabbed me. "How about a little morning adventure?"

"First of all there is nothing 'little' about an adventure with you. But this morning we are going to solve the case of the amnesiac waiter."

"Did you learn something?"

"Let's just say I'm on to something big."

"I've got something big for you."

"Get up and get dressed," I said. "We're going to Ruby's for breakfast."

The three of us were showered and shaved and ready for breakfast as we headed to Ruby's. Argus and Sparky had been fed and they curled up on the bed for a morning nap. We arrived at Ruby's just as it was opening.

"You guys are early," said Skippy as he took us to a table and poured our coffee.

"I need a recent picture of you?" I said as I took out my cell phone and took a snap shot of him. "I also need a picture of the cross you wear." Skippy took out his cross and I took a close up photo of it.

"What's all this about?" he asked.

"We are hot on the trail of your identity," said Hugh. "Jesse thinks he's on to something."

"What is it?" he asked with real excitement in his voice.

"I don't want to get your hopes up," I explained, "but I think the cross might be the clue to who you are."

"This?" he said holding the cross up. "I don't even know why I have it."

"I think I do," I said with more confidence than I felt. What if I'm wrong? "Any way, we all need a good breakfast."

"I'm going into the kitchen and make you a great breakfast casserole," he said as he skipped off to the kitchen.

I was in the office uploading a photograph of the cross. Black Broker does have a photo recognition setting, but it works for faces, not objects. I did feed the description of the cross into the program. The cross was ornate with symbols, but I had no idea what those symbols meant, if anything.

I left the program to grind away, while I went down the street to the coffee shop to grab some doughnuts, and four cups of coffee. I could have made coffee in the break room, but I was too keyed up to concentrate on much.

"Hey, Jesse, how's life?" asked Bryan Stillwater as he boxed up a dozen tasty doughnuts and half gallon of coffee in a container with a handle.

"You know how it goes, you get kicked down and you get up again."

"Isn't that the truth," he said as I handed over the money and picked up the goodies.

It hadn't taken Sparky long to learn from Argus. Both pugs were sitting under the table in the break room as we consumed the coffee and doughnuts. "So tell me why you think the cross is significant," said Hugh.

"Because so far that's the only unique clue we have," I answered. "Crosses like that aren't something you pick up in a jewelry store, hence it must have some religious significance."

"That makes sense," agreed Tim. "But it seems to be a hybrid type of cross."

"Hybrid?" asked Hugh.

"More than a plain cross, but not a crucifix, either," he answered.

Looking confused, Jessica said, "I don't get it?"

"A cross is plain," I said. "To Protestants the empty cross represents the risen Jesus. A crucifix has the body of Jesus still on the cross to represent sacrifice. Crucifixes are favored by the more traditional denominations, like Roman Catholics and Episcopalians. Skippy's cross had an image of Jesus surrounded by what looks like light, and he is holding up his hand in a blessing."

"So what does the cross tell us about his religious affiliation?" asked Hugh.

"I've no idea," I admitted. "It's just something I'm going to follow up on." My plan was to check out my idea by myself. If I was right then I could solve the case. If not I'd lose credibility. At least that's what I believed.

After the break I returned to my office and saw that Black Broker had ground to a halt and spit out information. As I scrolled through the results I saw a page with various types of crosses on it. I looked and there it was in full color. It was an exact representation of Skippy's cross. All of the clues fit together. "I'm so stupid," I said aloud. "It was all there and I didn't see it. I bet a ten-year-old could have solved this case. "I'm going to follow up on a hunch," I said to everyone. "I'll be away for a day or two. Take good care of the dogs. I'll let you know if anything pans out."

"You want one of us to go with you?" asked Tim.

"No, I best check this out alone. Besides I have a feeling we'll be getting another case soon."

I said my good byes, grabbed a travel case I keep packed in my office, and headed to my car.

It was going to be a long drive as I headed to upstate New York. I picked up route one in Bath and merged onto route I-95 in Topsom, and picked up the Maine turnpike just outside of Portland.

I did stop in Freeport for a little break. Wandering through L.L. Bean's gave me the opportunity to pick up a few more items of clothing for my travels. I had lunch at the Jameson Tavern and continued on my way.

Crossing the bridge in Portsmouth I was well on my way to picking up Interstate I-495 headed to Worchester and picked up I-90 into New York and continued on to the Hudson Valley.

I'm not one who loves to drive for hours on end, so when I reached my destination I checked into my motel room, unpacked, and took a nap.

Chapter 36

It was early morning and out here in the country I could hear the birds singing as the sun came up. I headed to the dining room and ordered a hearty breakfast because I wasn't sure how my day was going. So far I was relying on my intuition believing I was on the right track but fearing that I might be wrong.

I looked at my watch and saw that it was too early to make a visit, so I decided to do some sightseeing. I got in the car and headed out not knowing or caring where I was going. I knew the GPS would rescue me if I got too lost. The geography was different from coastal Maine. I stopped at a scenic turnout and took some photos. Before I knew it my watch said it was ten-thirty, and I set the GPS to my destination and was surprised that I was less than five miles away.

In no time at all I was at a stone arch proclaiming The Community of the Holy Spirit. It was just as I pictured it with rolling hills along the river with several large buildings of stone. Off in the distance were the vineyards just as I expected.

Skippy's cross was in the design of the monastery's brotherhood. This was an Episcopal monastery for men, founded more than a hundred years ago. I parked my car in the lot marked for visitors and headed up to the ornate main building. There was a huge oak door that looked like it would be almost too heavy to move. I rang the bell and waited. Slowly the door swung open confirming my belief that the door was indeed heavy. Standing in the doorway was a young man in his twenties wearing a brown habit with a hood. It was the brown hoodie that Skippy had seen in his dreams.

"Welcome," said the young man. "I'm Brother Timothy. How may we be of service?"

"My name is Jesse Ashworth and I'm a private detective. I'm chasing down the lead of a missing person, and I was hoping someone here could help."

"Let me take you to Father Brian. He's our Superior." The young monk picked up the phone and made a call. "Come this way."

I was led down a long hallway and up a set of stairs and into a large office with a great view of the river. Father Brian was somewhere in his fifties and had a kindly look to him."

"Welcome Mr. Ashworth. I understand we might be able to help you." He got up from behind his desk, shook my hand, and then we sat down in a small seating area.

"I have a client who is suffering from amnesia. He has hired my office to search for his true identity. My search has taken me here."

"Indeed," he said looking puzzled.

"Have you seen this man?" I asked passing him the photograph. As he looked at the photo the color drained from his face.

"He's alive?"

"Very much so. He calls himself John Smith."

"Praise God! We were afraid he was dead. His real name is Peter Bradley. He was Brother Peter. He was our cook and an excellent one at that. What happened?"

"As far as the police were able to piece together he was the victim of a hit and run in Portland, Maine. He was found in a ditch and taken to the hospital. He has been unable to remember his formal life. He is living in Bath, Maine as a waiter and a cook at Ruby's restaurant."

"Brother Peter had gone on a sabbatical to visit family members. He has an elderly aunt in Portland. When he didn't return we called his family, but no one had seen him. We reported Brother Peter missing, but I'm afraid the police believed he just wanted to disappear from the monastery."

"If I could have a list of his family members that would be helpful," I requested.

"Of course. What do you intend to do if I may ask?"

"I will, of course, tell him what I have learned. It may or may not jog his memory. What he does with the information will be up to him." I could hear bells off in the distance.

"That is the call for midday prayers. Please join us and stay for lunch. It will give us a chance to talk."

"I would like that," I said and followed Father Brian off to the chapel.

Back at home I hadn't said anything to Skippy. I wanted to make sure my hunches were correct. Now that I had answers I wasn't sure how to break the news to him.

"Invite him over for dinner," suggested Tim. "We can break the news slowly. After all. Imagine what it would be like to learn who you are."

"If anyone should know," I said remembering that Tim had suffered amnesia as a result of a brain tumor, "it would be you."

Skippy showed up for dinner that night and Hugh acted as bar tender. "Skippy," I said as he sat down with his drink. "Our investigation is complete."

"You know who I am?" he asked and I realized how unusual a case this was.

"Yes, here is the file for you to read," I said as I passed him the case file I had typed up.

He looked at the unopened folder. "I'm afraid to look."

"There is nothing bad in that folder. Maybe a surprise or two."

Slowly he opened the folder. I tried to read his emotions, but his face remained blank. He looked stunned, and why wouldn't he?"

"It's all there," I said. "A record of your life up until your accident. There is also a list of your family members."

"Some things look familiar," he said slowly. "At least now my dreams make sense."

"Take it slowly," said Tim. "Take your time with all this."

"Could I have another drink?" he asked as he finished his glass of wine.

I passed him the wine bottle. It was a bottle that Father Brian had given me from their very own vineyard. Skippy, or rather Peter Bradley, looked at the bottle and some sort of emotion passed across his face.

"I've seen this before," he said as he turned the bottle over and over in his hand.

"I think, Peter," I said using his real name for the first time, "it's time for dinner."

Weeks later Skippy was still working as the cook at Ruby's. He had taken Tim's advice and moved forward slowly. He had gone off to visit the monastery for a weekend and had contacted his family members. Parts of his memory had been restored, and some things still were missing.

"I've decided," Skippy said to us one morning when we were having breakfast at Ruby's. "that I like my life here. I don't think I'll ever remember everything, but I've built a new life here and I like it."

"I'm glad you're staying," I said. "And as you know you are always welcomed at our home."

"Home," he repeated. "Yes, home. My home is here now. And as someone once said 'Home is the very best place.'"

The End

Hawaiian Holiday

One Pot Pasta

Italian grandmothers everywhere are turning over in their graves, but this is tasty and requires no boiling of pasta.

Ingredients
1 lb. lean ground beef
1 sweet onion, diced minced
2 3/4 c. water
15 oz. canned tomato sauce
15 oz. canned diced tomatoes, drained
1 tbsp. dried Italian seasoning
1 tsp. salt
1 tsp. black pepper
1/2 tbsp. sugar
12 oz. spaghetti
1/2 c. grated Parmesan
2 tbsp. chopped parsley

Directions
In a large pot over medium-high heat, add beef, onion, and cook until beef is cooked through. Be sure to drain the fat. Add water, tomato sauce, diced tomatoes, Italian seasoning, salt, pepper, and sugar. Bring to a boil over high heat. Break spaghetti noodles in half and add to pan. Reduce heat to a simmer and cover. Cook, stirring often, until noodles are cooked through, 12 to 15 minutes. Sprinkle parmesan cheese before serving

Spam and Cabbage Stir Fry

Ingredients:

1 can of spam diced
1 half onion diced
1 medium cabbage sliced thin
3 tbsp of soy sauce

Directions:

Add all ingredients into large wok or fry pan. Cook until cabbage is soft, but not mushy.

Spam and Egg Casserole

Ingredients:

Tater Tots about 32 oz
One dozen Eggs
1 cup whipped cream cheese
1/3 cup light cream
1 can of spam diced
2 cups shredded chedder cheese
2 tsp seasoned salt

Directions:

Preheat oven to 400.
Grease a 9X13 pan and place half the tater tots on the bottom of the pan. In a large bowl beat eggs, whipped cream cheese and cream. Add cubed spam and 1 cup of cheese. Spoon egg bake mixture into the top of half of the tater tots. Top mixture with remaining tater tots and seasoning salt, bake for 1 hour. Remove from oven and top with remaining cheese, return to oven and bake an additional 5 minutes.

Hawaiian Barbecue Pulled Chicken Sandwiches

Slow cooking chicken in pineapple sauce adds a unique flavor to this dish.

Ingredients:
2 cups pineapple juice
1 cup brown sugar
3/4 cup ketchup
1 tablespoon soy sauce
1 1/2 teaspoons Worcestershire sauce
1 teaspoon salt
1/2 teaspoon pepper
1/2 teaspoon onion powder
1/2 teaspoon ginger
2 tablespoons butter
3 pounds boneless, skinless chicken breasts
1 cup chopped onion
1/4 cup flour

Directions:
Fry onions. Place all ingrediants except chicken in a bowl and mix. Place all ingredients in slow cooker and cook on low 6 to 8 hours or on high for 3 to 4 hours

Pork Tenderloin with Apples Recipe

Ingredients:

1 pork tenderloin
Salt and pepper
2 teaspoons ground cumin
2 apples sliced and peeled

Directions:

Preheat oven to 400° F.   Brown the pork loin in fry pan
.Cut pork loin halfway down the length of the meat. Place
apple slices in the cut. Season with salt, pepper and bake
until an internal temperature of 145

Hawaiian Holiday

Hawaiian Holiday

Made in the USA
Columbia, SC
04 January 2019